WALK SOFTLY ON THIS
HEART OF MINE

WALK SOFTLY ON THIS HEART OF MINE

a novel

CALLIE COLLINS

DOUBLEDAY
NEW YORK
2025

Published by Doubleday, a division of Penguin Random House LLC,
1745 Broadway, New York, NY 10019.

DOUBLEDAY and the portrayal of an anchor with a dolphin are registered
trademarks of Penguin Random House LLC.

Book design by Casey Hampton

LCCN 2024021045
ISBN 978-0-385-54884-7
Ebook ISBN 978-0-385-54885-4

penguinrandomhouse.com | doubleday.com

PRINTED IN THE UNITED STATES OF AMERICA

1 3 5 7 9 10 8 6 4 2

The authorized representative in the EU for product safety and compliance is
Penguin Random House Ireland, Morrison Chambers, 32 Nassau Street,
Dublin D02 YH68, Ireland, https://eu-contact.penguin.ie.

For Austin, Texas—

dust to dust, baby.

The reputation for tolerance is what got a lot of people here. We had people showing up at the Armadillo that had heard this was a city of like-minded souls. They were getting whacked by rubber hoses at home, so they came here to simply find a more tolerant atmosphere. In some people's minds, tolerance is mistaken for something benign, but it's not.

—EDDIE WILSON

He says, "Boy, what you gonna do
With your heart in two?"

—JASON MOLINA, "JOHN HENRY SPLIT MY HEART"

We'd had the bar half as long as we'd been married, and so about fifteen years, when our regulars started to disappear. We weren't worried at first. Or not too worried, really. The guy with the scar along his jawline and the silly Stetson who would bring all his girls—sit across from them and rub his hands together over the table like he was warming them over a fire—didn't show up for weeks, but we assumed he must've moved away. Fewer parties though too. Not even our friends came around as often. It got so that between open and when the music started, only two or three people would wander in. They'd usually be alone, or with a single friend, and they would sit with them all intimately, forehead to forehead and their backs hunched on the round stools, interested only in each other. What I mean is that they could've been anywhere at all, in any room in any town in the world. And they'd order beers or shots of Beam and drink them so slowly Wendell could wash the glasses one by one in the back only every thirty minutes, could even take his time with them—if he ever took his time with anything—and we'd never get backed up at all. And then one Friday night we realized it'd been a whole week since we'd had to make last call. Wendell would just walk through the white noise of the jukebox speakers when it felt late enough, kick away the brick, pull closed the front door, and flip the dead bolt. All at once our customers seemed to dissolve back into the woods around us, like a sinkful of water slipping down a drain. Suddenly it was just dry.

And the music didn't start until late, usually. Until at least nine. The weekend sets didn't even bring out a crowd anymore. Darrell and his band had been playing Fridays and Saturdays as long as we could remember, but they hadn't seemed to write anything or even learn a tune that hadn't been in the set already in years, felt like. And if there was anyone still left in the room past the last jangly chord and down-strum of "I Saw the Light," they'd swivel toward whoever was tending bar and signal gently, just a little flick of a hand in the air, for their tab. No one danced. The floors were clean of boot scuffs even, and I came out of the kitchen one night to find Wendell moving around the room like a weird sort of cowboy puppet, janky and as close as he gets to ashamed, planting one foot and scraping his other toe in a long, loud path behind him, over and over again.

It used to be that it didn't matter what we did, who we booked—the place would be full. So hot inside in the summers that we could feel the sweat coming off folks from two feet behind the bar; it'd soak right up into the air and settle back down on our skin, mingle with our own. By eight thirty Wendell and I would both look like we'd stepped directly out of a shower. We'd leave the back door wide open, and the side door too, and people would cluster around them frenzied, burst out into the parking lot like herds of animals, trying to catch any kind of breeze. Ashtrays, always endless ashtrays to empty, full of the sooty remains of Parliaments and skinny 100's, and the tables sticky with the yellow of cedar pollen when it was falling. In the winters a different kind of heat, a big warmth, the bar glowing gold every night like midnight mass on Christmas Eve and full of booze. And it did feel somehow religious, I'd thought. Full of a stranger, bigger kind of faith than the one I knew. When Wendell set up chairs, I sometimes even thought of them as pews. The pool table a sort of altar covered in its plastic tarp and scattered, chipped glasses and extra cables coiled tight like snakes. Sometimes even the guitars, together and wailing, sounded to me like they were praying.

Where was everybody now? we'd asked each other. *And what could we do?* Even Wendell—who used to be so light and real easy in the eyes, would duck his whole tall body under the bar door and pop back up on the other side like he'd done some kind of magic—looked crushed. I felt a creeping kind of lonely I hadn't known in a long time. When I'd get in the car at the end of the night, the building looked dark as sin, like someone had boarded it up, and the air felt stifling. The big, white neon star on the front of the bar shone like the moon, and the blank sky pushed down on us, mean and surely on purpose—I told Wendell—between the trees. We couldn't afford much more of the quiet in a strict financial sense either. We were paying higher bills on Rush Creek than we should've been, considering how far out of town it was. But the lot was big, and there was the house on the other side, and the foundations were cracking along with the limestone underneath them. The power could be finicky in the wrong weather, and if it got cold for more than a day or two in January, the heat would go out, and it'd just stay cold until we bugged the hell out of the city, until they sent a guy out to get down on his knees and rattle his hands around in the vents.

So Wendell and I made a plan. I'd hold down the fort alone, pay Darrell only a portion of the tips for playing the same country covers every night, take his hard look all on my own, and Wendell would go out to scout for somebody new to play, someone who could bring people out again. It took months. Alone in the bar I would get bored and wound-up. Angry, even, at having ended up where I had. I'd fly into fantasies of crowds and sound while I wiped down the tables for the seventh time, the eighth. Crowds and sound were all I wanted. I was still here, sure, but wilted and wounded, back against the wall. And when Wendell would come home at the end of the night, he didn't much have it in him to talk, would just slip off his jeans over his thick socks and sleep nearly silent. He'd come back with Jack breath and slow feet and darker, lazy eyelids. But then, eventually, he came back with Doug.

Do I wish I could go back in time and change what happened? Just pull the emergency brake and stop the whole goddamn thing before it had even started? Do I wish Wendell hadn't been at the Armadillo that night and seen Doug play and set all of our lives in motion again? I don't really know. I do know that a still life—a mind in too much quiet—can be a dangerous thing. And I have to live with the long echo of the choices I made, and maybe, mostly, the choices I didn't. But I don't see much value anymore in looking backward. Better some noise—right? in the end?—than nothing at all.

all right, then, fuck it,
on my count, boys,
and that's a real short one, two,

ONE	1
TWO	99
THREE	171

and

ONE

We moved out to Rush Creek for the job. The house was just a bonus. I hadn't had a solid gig for months on end, and the offer Wendell made me the night I met him was almost too good to believe. I didn't even really expect anything from the house, the way he kind of glossed over it. But it was huge, old, and kinda out of place, like it'd been lifted right off a farm in Carolina or somewhere in the Deep South. A big front porch and the living room full of sun from the windows. It was crumbling some, sure, and the upstairs was just these dusty, cramped bedrooms off a low landing that sloped sideways, and some of the floorboards had curled and split. He told us we could live in it as long as we wanted. Like it would've been *want*. Nah. It was need. And the kid had space to run around and woods like I had when I was little, out behind the old place in San Antonio, in Beacon Hill, and it was strange, truly, living in such weird rickety luxury and in such close proximity to where I played. It made me feel somehow like I finally got a real life. A real job with real hours and real pay, even though it was none of those things when you really examined the situation. I was

3

just playing guitar like always and singing to some people in a place that smelled like cigarettes and white vinegar, and still on bar hours while Julian slept and Gwen smoked and read out on the goddamn veranda—the veranda, she called it—and watched the cars pull in and out of the parking lot that separated the house from the bar like toys, Hot Wheels. What cash I made came to me sweaty and rolled up in wads that felt as big as baseballs rubber-banded in my palm. I told Gwen that whatever else she was missing out here, the pay didn't get much realer than that.

I was writing too, finally, but not the way I was used to. I'd play an old song until I was so bored the words were just coming out of my mouth while my head was somewhere else, until my fingers rubbed the neck and skipped the frets like they were someone else's fingers, but somehow in that space of nothingness a new idea would come to me. My hand would be moving from that downhearted-sounding E with the loud hammer into the fifth and back down the neck, but in my mind I'd get a snatch of a new song in B-flat, a little quick twelve-bar like Louis would play in the basement of Donn's when I was fifteen and trying to act like I knew what I was doing. Just a little twelve-bar. Easy stuff, but at least it was new. The old couch so soft you could fall right through it and the high ceiling beams up above me like they were listening.

I hadn't had new in a long while, and without new I hadn't had anything. Everyone could see it. And I felt it when I played, a still and stiff feeling, like my life wasn't gassed up anymore but just stalled out on a short stage in a shitty room, only a foot up above the ground, and the swelled opening of "Goin' Down Slow" just stretching out long like a record, echoing around and with no rhythm even. An early show every week at the Armadillo. Benny doing octaves on the upright and Hopper on the drums behind me, but all of it kind of floating in space. More low nights like those, I had sworn to myself, and I'd have given Gwen what I thought she wanted. Given up the old Capitol deal that I knew wasn't ever gonna pan out anyway, and the measly royalty checks from that one tune they'd put out on a label compilation that couldn't even cover half the groceries, and I woulda found my way to a real day's work. That's how she called it, *a real day's work*. And maybe she was right. Maybe after that real day's work, I could look my kid in the eyes. Buy him what he wanted, which used to be a trampoline for the yard and now apparently new pairs of jeans or a puppy and the food to feed it or somewhat. More low nights like I'd been having before Rush Creek and I'd have known that I was meant to give in.

But after only a couple days in the house, I was happier. I thought I was finally getting it back. I wasn't there yet exactly. It was such better digs than I'd ever lived in—lord, we'd come straight from that true shithole on Chicon, where Gwen spent all her time worrying about who was coming out of the alley behind the complex. The music was better on the east side, but she wasn't having it. She did have a whole new host of worries out here, like she said. The house was this sprawling thing, with some of those upstairs rooms in pretty bad shape, and the ceiling was bowed like God himself had been loafing on it. The carpets were burned in places, and the sink in the kitchen barely trickled, and I could tell there were animals living underneath it when I bent down to listen to the pipes. There was a hole in the ceiling of the dining room, so when I sat at the table I could see straight up into the roof. I wasn't gonna have enough money to fix any of it, at least not anytime soon. Was it even ours to fix? I felt too sheepish to ask. And out back behind us was the woods, like I said. Gwen was right that we were at least a couple miles farther west of the heart of the city than Wendell had hinted to me we'd be.

Wendell, who'd shown up at the Armadillo one night when we had some sort of groove going and people stood up in the middle of "Laredo," like any of them had been down 35 that far. The thing about singing songs about real Texas to these fake Texans was that when they got into something and really latched on and started to dance and move and I could hear some pop in the shuffle, I couldn't feel anything but angry and alone. It was a night when I couldn't remember why I'd moved to Austin, and then—even after it didn't work the first time—had moved back again. It was a night when I couldn't remember why I'd married Gwen, why I'd let her have a baby, egged her on even when she got the idea a little too early, when I was still seeing Kathleen but not often, only when she showed up at the after-parties at Ben Lamb's. Anyway, it was one of those nights that Wendell came in. After the set, Hopper was breaking down the snares and tucking the stands into the felt of their cases. He touched his drums so gracefully and carefully I sometimes wondered if he thought they had feelings, but he does everything like that. I was packing up my guitar. Wendell came up and said something cheesy and awkward like, "Great set, y'all, really killer."

And I said something like, "Felt good tonight, thanks, man." I was still packing up the gear and didn't have it in me.

But from behind me he said, "Doug," and it was so strange and sudden to hear a man I'd never seen call my name in that serious way Wendell has that I stopped what I was doing. He said, "I think I got a gig for you."

"And who're you, bud?" I asked, but I didn't want to be too eager or weird about it, so I didn't even turn around. Tony walked by to grab some gear, a pedal he wanted to borrow for the next set.

"A guy who's got a gig for you," he said.

"What gig you got? Where's this gig?" I asked, but then I closed the case and flipped the locks and turned and was looking at him suddenly, really looking at him, for the first time.

"I have a thing going here, you can tell," I said, which was mostly a lie.

"I have a proposition," he said, and a smile started to spread across his face, and he looked a little bit desperate but also somehow serious as a judge. Maybe so serious, I realize now, 'cause of being so desperate. "I want to book you every night, till the end of the summer at least, and I even got a place for you to live too."

And there was just no way in hell that was true, I thought, but it occurred to me to pry at it a little, so I said, "Uh-huh, man. How much a night?"

"Come see the place," he said. "I'm Wendell, that's my name."

"It's not just me, you know. If you're not full of shit about a place to live. I got a wife and a kid. What kind of place?"

"A house," he said. "Just come out and see it tomorrow."

"What's the catch here?" I lowered my voice a little. "And how come I've never heard of you, Wendell? That's a weird name, and this is a small town," I said, I think, and I finally took my eyes off his face and looked down at his boots. I could tell they were real boots, had been worn for years and maybe even to do work, and not the fancy ones the kids buy down at Allens and then shove into the back of their closets until they want to go out and dance and play like cowboys and always half ironic. There was dirt on them. Not quite red clay as if he'd really walked off a ranch, but clots of dark mud on the heels and dust on the toes.

"No catch," he said. "It's a good gig. I'll pay you good money for it. I have a bar just west a little, I've had it for a long time, and there's a house next to it, and I want you to be the house band, you and your boys."

"The house band?"

"The house band," he said.

"They're not always my boys," I said, and this tall guy calling Benny and Hopper and whoever else my boys made me want to laugh, and I did.

"I bet they would be if you got them a permanent house gig, won't they?" he asked, and I probably sort of nodded then through my chuckling.

"How far west we talking here? I'm not trucking way the hell out for nothing."

"Just come and see it, I'll drive you out," he said, not offended in the damn least, and I said OK, I would.

Couldn't hurt, I figured. Plus, I was drunk. He looked so pleased I laughed again, and so did he.

And yeah, I told people back then, Wendell does make an impression at first. It's not like he's even half as strange once you get to know him. He is tall, yeah sure, but man, the tallness you can get used to pretty quickly. I will admit that the first time he picked Jules off the ground and put him up on his shoulders, my heart did a quick little stutter, but that's purely biological. I'm normal height, and so is Gwen. *Who's this tall man taking our kid away?* is what my biology was saying. But it's not the height that makes Wendell so nervous-making. It's something in the eyes, and the hands, and the way he walks kind of like he's not totally in control of his body, and the way he talks real close to you, and how he can get too worked up about small things and not worked up enough about the big ones, kind of like he's not totally in control of his mind either. Sometimes I've thought he doesn't belong in this town at all, even at his bar in the woods, but he had set his mind to filling the place for him and Deanna, and who was I to deny him that real simple dream, especially when I needed it too. And who was anybody to deny me mine.

Wendell picked me up the next day in the parking lot of the Armadillo, and the sun was coming out from behind the buildings and steaming up the pavement even though it was only April. My jeans were damp and sticky behind my knees. I got in his truck, and he reversed out of the lot right back onto First, into traffic like it was nothing, even though the lot was a circle and he could've eased his way into the street. People swerved around us and glared. He didn't seem to mind in the least. There are a lot of guys in Austin who don't seem to get that it's 1975 and not 1950, that there are people here now and lots of 'em, but it was kinda charming anyway to watch him. And he talked constantly, the whole way west, with downtown getting smaller in the side mirror, and then he turned up a road I didn't know and just kept on talking, talking about music like someone who doesn't know music, and then when I wasn't too receptive to that he started telling me about the town, how it'd been before, like I didn't know. Everybody knows. Fuck, it's all people talk about.

He drawled his a's longer and flatter than most of the guys I knew, including the ones who'd grown up out west, and I wondered but didn't ask where he was from. I listened, and I liked Wendell, even though half of what came out of his mouth was absolute bullshit. Maybe I liked him a little more for it. I didn't even want to correct the things I knew he was getting wrong—what December it was when Albert was playing that show at Flossie's and shit went scary and that girl got cut accidentally, which corner Lung's had been on before they'd torn it down. All I wanted was to see Wendell's place and hear the details. Gwen had asked me that morning to pay particular attention to the details of the arrangement, and I'd asked if she wouldn't just like to come along, then, since she was apparently in the band now and could gauge a good gig and check out acoustics and feel as well as I could, asked her if I wasn't just pretty much disposable at this point, and she'd soured then and made me promise to at least get a firm handshake on the living agreement.

"I guess you'd want to know some specifics?" Wendell asked, after a pause, like he'd been listening to me thinking. In the back of the cab a couple of empty bottles slammed together and rang out so loud that I reached my arm back there and grabbed one of them—as Wendell took a curve it rolled into my hand—and I tossed it up onto the seat.

"I mean, sure, yeah."

"And you'd want to get the drummer and the other fella up here to check out the bar, likely?"

"The other fella." I laughed. "Benny's one of the best guitar players in this goddamn town," I said, which wasn't an exaggeration. Actually it made me feel bad how good Benny was—and I was worried he knew it, even though I'd always hidden it best I could. But he couldn't sing for absolute shit, and I was grateful for that.

"Anyway," I said, "they'll let me make the call."

We'd come to a long driveway, wide like a road but gravel and all rutted out, real rough, and Wendell took a sharp right into it. My ass came up off the seat.

"I'll pay y'all real well," Wendell said. "We've been having a hard time getting people out at the bar lately, I don't really know what happened. Used to be we were packed."

I almost made a dumb crack about the road—made sense that people stopped coming if they couldn't even *get* to the damn bar—and way out here too, when the party was more downtown than it'd ever been. But then we came up to the parking lot and the house on the left of it rising like a whole ghost mansion out of the heat. Wendell pointed the other direction out of the truck, though.

"There it is," he said. "That's the bar."

So, OK. I got my bearings. Around the buildings and all through the lot there were trees—or what we call trees, even though they ain't full trees really, just bushes with complexes—sprouting up everywhere. I could see three old live oaks in random spots around the dirt lot, and I could imagine what a nightmare it made the parking if it ever was really crowded like he'd said. I trained my eyes on the bar so as to fight the urge to just sit there staring at the house like a moron.

The bar was newer than the house, but still, the joint looked worn-out. It was a concrete box of a building with a flat roof and flat walls and flat everything, so flat it looked almost like an adobe you could find a few hundred miles west or south. The sign on the front read RUSH CREEK SALOON in giant letters. *These fucking guys and their saloons around here*, I thought. *We're in a goddamn city even if it doesn't feel like it sometimes. Saloons are for movies or New Mexico or somewhat.* This was a bar.

Wendell swung the truck in right up front, and I slid out. And then there was enough dust in the place that I could feel it in my nose when Wendell opened the door, so I knew immediately that people hadn't really been coming out for longer than he'd even made it seem. Some chairs were stacked neatly in a corner, and I wondered how long it'd been since anyone unstacked them. It smelled cleaner than a bar should smell, even though it had gotten hot early that spring. It smelled like no one'd spilled beer or taken a piss in this building in years. Along one of the walls was a string of orange Texas pennants that kind of flapped in the breeze of a giant box fan they had going in one of the corners. The floor was wooden and led up to a small stage clean of instruments or gear or anything besides an upright tucked against a wall and a tattered old dime-store rug. The stage was barely big enough to fit a four-piece, but Wendell saw me looking at it and quickly swore it was better than it looked and we'd be fine and happy up there, the sound was real good, and he told me I was welcome to get up and play to test out the space.

But then, suddenly, there was Deanna. Deanna, walking toward me. She's a hard one to describe dead-on. Deanna's a real good girl somehow, a woman, yeah, but a good girl too, and I could tell that right away, swear to God, right when I stepped into the bar and squinted through the dark to see the little stage and the big floor and tables so cheap they'd collapse under four good fingers of whiskey, and caught sight of her making her way through the doorway out of the kitchen with a rag in her hand. It was so nice to see a woman. I realized that I'd been the tiniest bit freaked during the drive out with Wendell that he was going to take me somewhere I didn't want to go and couldn't make my way out of. I didn't know the guy from Adam, really, and I could hold my own if

I needed to, but I was as skinny then as I am now and always at least a little conscious of the size of the folks around me. I had the kind of personal awareness of someone who stands out in a crowd of people, or most crowds of people anyway, 'cause growing up, I did. Stand out. And that feeling was real hard to shake, even after everybody started dressing and talking like I did, letting their hair get a little wild and going out in sandals.

I looked around the room, and my eyes had adjusted, and I could see more clearly now. Deanna came closer to me, tossed the rag from her right hand to her left, and reached out to shake mine, said hello.

"Hey," I said back.

For a minute we were both silent.

"Well," I started to say, and she said, "Oh! I'm Deanna, I'm Wendell's wife."

"Pleasure," I said.

"And you're the musician?" she asked, dropped my hand, and very fast wiped hers on the thigh of her jeans, which made me conscious of my own sweaty palms, and I felt down and gross next to her. She was in this white T-shirt, I remember.

I saw Wendell out of the corner of my eye. He had this way of walking; he kind of lumbered, like a lanky gorilla swinging his arms, but fast too, and he made his way like that down a small hallway to the right of the stage.

"Yes. A musician, yes, ma'am."

"Oh, don't do that," Deanna said. "I can't be that much older than you are."

15

"Habit, sorry," I mumbled, and felt like a little kid. There was something about the whole day that was throwing me off, but not in an all-terrible way.

I met her eyes. In the light of the room they were almost black, and I wondered how old she was. Forty, maybe? Forty-five?

"Doug Moser," I remembered to say suddenly, and she smiled wide.

"Really happy to have you here, Doug Moser," she said.

It made me blush.

"How long have you——" I started, but I didn't even get to finish my question before Wendell came back down the hall. A door slammed closed somewhere behind him, and he had the neck of a shitty Squier Strat in one hand and the other was carrying a little amp not by the handle on top but like a baby in a hold. He had to stoop awkwardly to set the amp down on the edge of the stage and plug in the cable, and he motioned at me with the guitar to come up there. I smiled at Deanna like to say sorry, but she was looking up at the stage too, her shoulders kinda slumped.

And as I got up to the front of the room and turned back around, I could feel that Wendell wasn't wrong about the sound. The bar spread out before me. I sat down on the stool next to the piano and took the guitar from him and propped up my right knee a little higher than my left and started to feel it out, slowly at first, made my way around the E arpeggios. It was a shit little guitar. Even as I played, it was dropping out of tune and sounded real flat when I came up into the A. I had to stop playing and retune. Deanna was looking at me and so was Wendell, and I remember wishing that the room were completely empty or completely full of people. I couldn't hear the sound with just me and two people watching. Nah, I thought, I'd tried, but no. Still I got the guitar settled down, and I made a quick decision and that decision was: what the hell, I was there anyway, and I started to really play, drove into something, I can't even remember what now, but I closed my eyes to hear better and I swear to God the bar lit up with noise. Like magic, it lit right up like magic. The notes felt right coming off the walls and down from the ceiling; they were real sugar, even though it was just a box and should've felt like a sealed-up echo chamber. Even though I was playing the world's shittiest electric and could almost feel the wiring inside of it spark against my leg.

"Yeah, baby," I said.

"All right?" Wendell asked.

I hit a harmonic and let it ring till it died out. "That's some room, you know? I can feel it all the way up to the ceiling," I said, and Wendell smiled so wide it was like somebody new had taken over his face.

"Your music is different," Deanna said, after a minute. "Is that how you always play?"

"It's blues," I said. "Kind of country, kind of the blues. A little soul. Well, it's closer to the blues than to anything else. Till we get Benny in here with the accordion, at least. Then I don't know what you call it."

"Blues," she said, like a mother playing along. "But you're—"

"White as can be? Yes, ma'am." Then: "Fuck, sorry."

17

She laughed then, loud, and my world stretched open a little wider.

"Good," she said. "I'm sick of the old shit."

"All right," Wendell said. He looked over at her, and then back to me with a huge smile on his mug.

"All right," he said again.

Hopper and Benny cheered me up the night they came out to bring most of the gear. I'd spent the day rebuilding the dresser we'd broken down to its pieces to get it to fit into my friend Phil's truck for the move, while Gwen pattered her way around the house putting things up. Trying to get a ten-year-old to hold a nail still was like trying to get the sun to shine in a storm—nothing doing—but Gwen was a nester. By the time evening rolled around, I needed something I could do right and so was grateful when I heard Benny's little VW scrape into the gravel lot. I lit a cigarette with the stove on my way out onto the porch, and Gwen looked at me like I'd killed somebody. I've always loved that girl, but I didn't know how I'd ended up so tied down that I couldn't even light a cigarette with my own gas.

"Saloon, asshole!" Benny yelled from the lot when I came out the front door.

The sun was setting the way it does sometimes, violently, and Benny's leather jacket shone purple under it. His hair was still dark from the winter, and it burst off his head like a mess of feathers. Benny's real small—five foot five maybe, on a good day, and thin as a piece of carbon copy—and he's spent his whole life pissed about it. He was wearing those skinny little plaid pants he loved, so tight I didn't know how he could walk in them. Plus, it was at least eighty out, close and wet. Hopper was pulling the van in next to Benny, and I came down the steps and walked the hundred feet to the cars.

"They don't know what they're getting out here, do they?" Benny said real loud.

"I think they know exactly what they got out here," Hopper said quieter, coming around the side of the van. He pried open the rusted double doors, rolled his big kick over the floorboard, out the side, and into his arms, squatted down low to catch it. "Be nice to leave some of the gear in one place anyway. They got a good lock on that closet, y'all think?"

I looked at him wide-eyed—I had no goddamn clue if there was a lock on the closet.

"OK, well, some help would also be nice."

"Explain to me again, Dougie," Benny said, "why you get to live out here in this house and we have to drive up *from* town every night and then drive our own asses *back* to town every night after that?"

"We're only ten minutes from the river, God. It ain't like it's far."

"Some help," Hopper said again. "If you'd ever like to get this done." He held the drum out in front of him like he was offering me a present and raised an eyebrow, and when I laughed he didn't but turned around instead and headed toward the bar. Benny grabbed the snare and a couple cases, and I turned to follow them the rest of the way through the lot with my smoke in my hand.

The truth was that I had worked pretty hard to get the guys to agree to drive out and play four times a week. I'd sworn up and down they'd get more than their share of the nightly, which wasn't bad—25 percent of the door on weekends and a guaranteed 20 bucks at least on slow nights—and I signed an actual contract with Wendell that said I wouldn't even pick up a guitar in any other joint for as long as he wanted. That in exchange for the house and the utilities, plus some amount of security and consistency and acting like I played for people when actually I'd always played for myself, when actually I was mostly just killing time until I figured out how to make what I did into what I wanted to do again.

Those months before Rush Creek weren't even when it'd been the hardest, though they hadn't been a fun ride, not at all. Nights at the Armadillo could go either way, and, at their best, people were filling the room up and the music had a glow and felt right when it dropped keys. My voice was hitting at the Armadillo too.

When had it been hardest? Before now, I mean. The hardest had been years ago, if I'm honest about it. After I'd left Gwen and Jules in Austin, after I'd gone out to LA for that half a year to try to make some moves and meet some people. I signed the recording deal one night in a booth at a too-bright club down a block or two from the Troubadour, and I really did think in that moment that I'd finally figured something out. But then I struck out with every Baja guitarist and drummer I liked in the whole goddamn town. I couldn't get the sound right at all, couldn't play anything well. I hated everybody I met, and I got so frustrated one night, alone with some snooty son-of-a-bitch engineer in the studio, that I dumped hot beer all over the carpet and ruined a few expensive pedals. I couldn't bring myself to go back the next day, so I loaded the truck under the dying palm tree in the apartment lot, and I came back home.

Jules was three and Gwen was wiped and Mama was sick, and suddenly I was back in the house off South Fifth, where water ran through the scrub woods, and all along it tarps and bottles and small campfires at night and the homeless cooking squirrels and basically living in our backyard, with all three of them. The place was way too small, and I didn't have the heart or the money to do anything about it. And then Mama came down with that last big cough, and the sixth or seventh time she coughed out blood with the gook, real blood I swear, unmistakable blood, bright red like paint, and I called the ambulance to come and then realized that we'd have to pay for it. In all the noise and fuss and my yelling, Gwen got upset and picked up the little ukulele from its stand—the only present my grandfather had ever given me—and brought it down like an ax into the coffee table. It splintered wide open. That was when it was the hardest.

I vowed to myself that I'd do whatever I had to do to avoid the feeling I had that night, listening to the siren come down the hill and looking at the split neck of the uke: a heavy certainty that all of life was just a bad joke, and then a very real longing to skip out before the punch line. Playing the 'Dillo once a week wasn't keeping me far enough from that feeling, and so it was important to me to convince Benny and Hopper that playing up here was a great opportunity, that it was worth a true shot.

"Dude, open the fucking door," Benny said to me under the front floodlight, his hands full of equipment. But I was flicking my butt out into the gravel, and Hopper adjusted the drum in his arms and opened it instead, with a little grunt and his hip. Benny and I went in after him.

Hopper set the kick down by a chair and walked immediately back out the door to the van. Hopper was cool, quiet and smooth. He was a real drummer, a good one who didn't need a lot of attention or talk to do his job and keep me and Benny straight. Hopper's focus and ease impressed the hell out of me, but it seemed to make Benny angry. Maybe he just resented Hopper for towering over him, or for the way Hopper would step in front of Benny when Benny got in too deep with somebody, or for the fact that Benny counted on Hopper to do it. Plus, I knew Benny was sick of crashing at Hopper's apartment, which he had to do because he spent all his cash on girls and never once the same one. Benny piled the cases in his hands on top of a table, looked around the room, and exhaled loud.

I was still trying to get a handle on the bar, and I'd spent some time paying attention to Wendell. He was from out west, it turned out, from up near Midland, and his family'd owned a big ranch, thousands of acres and heads of cattle too, and he shuffled and cracked sometimes like a ranch boy, though Deanna confided in me later that no matter how bad his father tried and urged him and whipped him, he'd been a truly terrible hand, and I could see that too. It was mostly in the way he lost track of his body and would always run into doorways, trip over chairs he didn't seem to need to be anywhere near. And for a barman, he sure spilled a lot of goddamn drinks, and particularly mine, it seemed. I try not to drink that much, but those first couple of weeks were what I'd call a transition period, and so I might've gone at it a little hard. And anyway, it was becoming clear to me that I was setting up shop in a country bar, a real honky-tonk out of different days, and that even though Wendell wanted me there, no one was going to know what to do with what I was playing now or with the groove.

Wendell must've been in the back of the bar 'cause he wasn't in the big room, but Deanna was, and I could see Benny kind of straighten when he spotted her plunging bottles into the ice behind the bar. The thing about Deanna is that she has these brown eyes that seem to look right into you, a deep soulful sort of dark look she gives you, and it's unsettling. Fifteen years younger and I'd never have left her alone, even if her husband was paying my bills. I got nervous when I talked to her. I thought her eyes were telling me half the time that she didn't really like me anyway, but I couldn't tell. If I thought about it, it was real essential to me that she *did* like me, which meant I also needed her to like Hopper and Benny.

She said hi to me when the door closed again behind Hopper, but she was looking at Benny a little unsure. She kept her eyes on him. Used to be I'd notice shit like that, but it didn't happen much anymore down at the clubs in town, where everybody looked the same, wore the same clothes, and moved the way we did. But up here I was aware of it, me with my long hair and Hopper, whose mama was Salvadoran, and Benny, who was the kind of absolute prick who enjoyed making people as edgy as he could, and I felt like a weird kid again, somehow snuck into a place I wasn't supposed to be. Benny noticed too, I could tell, and if he had any part of the feeling I was having it was bound to upset him, and right on cue he started playing it up with her, said, "Hey, baby, ¿qué onda?" with kind of a sexy swing in it.

"Sorry?" she asked real soft.

I could've kneecapped him.

"Just saying hello there," Benny said, and looked at her, and I could tell he was going to take it easy instead. Thank God.

"This is Benny, Deanna. Think we could get a few shots while we move the stuff in?"

"I'll take a beer too, but none of that American shit, if you please, thank you, darling," Benny said, and smiled.

"Thanks, Deanna," I said as nice as I could, but I could feel my teeth clench and my jaw get tight as soon as I was done with the words. Her cheeks were red and so was her neck, so red I could see it in the bar's low light, red all the way down to the low collar of her tank top, and she bowed her head and pulled a Heineken out of the trough so fast that little chunks of ice flung up around her.

"Hey," Hopper said when he came back in, went up to the stage to swivel the snare stand together, "let's go."

It's almost funny to remember that night now. Me, standing alone next to the pool table with the felt all ripped up and a chunk of the railing missing, looking at Deanna and thinking without thinking about what sort of tits were underneath her tank top. Benny's asshole smile, still going. Hopper organizing his set and grunting commands to himself on the small stage. No one in the bar except us, even though technically it was open. No cars in the lot even. And Deanna back there counting the well and working hard not to look at any of us, nervous or lonely or excited or ashamed, or a combination of all of them. What do you call the combination of all those feelings? The blues, man, don't you? I call it the blues anyway.

If the emptiness had been all I had to deal with at Rush Creek, I'd have been a luckier man. There I was in that moment just thinking that it'd be nice to have a place to play, and that it could be simple out here, that maybe I'd found the way into the kind of simple life I thought I might want, especially since I got back from California with nothing all over again. And maybe out here in the woods Gwen would be happier and Jules would be happier. I really did let myself believe that all I'd have to deal with were some good ole boys heckling us for a couple weeks, maybe. Or a month or two for Deanna to realize that Benny wasn't so awful after all, or that he was even worse than she expected but in a charming kind of way. Wendell's awkward encouragement, the way he peered at me like I was something besides a guy who played music. I was worried about all this, and about things like the dresser back in the house, whether I could keep the drawers from sticking. I was worried about the dumbest shit then. It might have been nice to have some true quiet, is what I'm saying. In that moment, I let myself imagine I could have some true quiet and that I could like it.

I first noticed the kid not too long after we started playing, only a couple weeks after the fliers went up downtown—

Doug Moser and the Good Goddamn
AKA the Lost Causes
AKA Bluesmen Extraordinares
Play at Rush Creek Saloon
Legendary Bar in the Woods
Saturday Night April 23
Come early for good seats

We were still trying to build up the crowd from the dead place Rush Creek had become, but so far the folks who were coming back were *coming back,* which means that they'd been around before, when Rush Creek was a hick bar and not a bar with me and the guys playing our weirdo blues rock, and it caught up to us that night I met Steven for the first time, caught up to me and Deanna and Wendell what kind of change we were making.

To be real honest, I'm not even sure we were *trying* to

make a change at all. I wasn't, at least. All Wendell had asked me to do was play music, and all I'd asked Hopper and Benny to do was play music with me, and Deanna hadn't really asked for anything at all except maybe for some people in the bar again so that she could keep it running and keep Wendell happy too. It wasn't this big thing. But it was true that the saloon sign outside Rush Creek had been realer than I'd thought. That old vibe was overwhelming at first. It made me jittery. I saw it in the way some of the people looked at us, like it was only a basic civility that kept them from yelling shit while we were on, or being real ugly to us after the set. But still somehow they listened, and hey, some of 'em danced, and they kept showing up.

I'd come over early that day to find Deanna sorting receipts and smiling to herself, swaying slightly to the juke. Both of the doors were propped wide open, and the sun was coming through them real pretty. In the lot the breeze was blowing all the sharp little leaves off the cedars, and the smell of cedar was all over the bar too, everything smelled like trees.

On its best days Rush Creek could feel half inside and half outside, and it was beautiful like that. There I was in that middle space, which is really the best thing about living in Texas, that afternoon time when there's nothing to do at all and no guilt in wasting it either. It's important to waste them, days like those. You never know when you're gonna get them. A group of people sat at one of the tables in the corner, drinking out of tall glasses, and the jukebox was going with old country but the good shit, early Waylon, and one of the women called out hi real kind to me when I moved into the room and toward the bar. T.K. was sitting at the bar rolling a smoke—it was a weekend, so at some point he'd palm a couple beers and post up on his stool by the door to take a cover. I said hey to him when I walked by, and Deanna heard me, looked up, and set her pencil down. She took out two glasses, and the light caught them and reflected sunny, shining spots onto the bar. She poured something, and she took a shot with me. I'd never seen her take a shot before, and she did it like no woman I've ever seen, stood up straight-backed and set her legs a little too far apart and gulped it fast and then slammed the glass down on the wood and smiled at me before grabbing both glasses with one hand and setting them in the rack. It was too sexy, too sexy. I looked at the backs of her arms, and they sagged a little but not too much. The whole scene warmed me up.

But for every moment like that one, there was a different kind of feeling, mostly late at night, after our sets were over and we broke down the equipment and waded into the crowd mixed together now and all of us three-sheets mostly. It was always easy to tell who had come to see us 'cause they'd seen the posters or heard from somebody, and who'd come because they'd known Rush Creek before and had heard something new was happening. Either way, people were coming out into the woods to drink again. Our people looked like us and could've easily come straight from Arlo's or the 'Dillo, and they sang along to everything, the big ones and the standards, knew our stuff. Those guys that Hopper played silly jazz with down in San Marcos came up some nights. They drank G&Ts, lit shitty joints under one of the oaks in the parking lot, crowded into a circle we'd drop into between sets. Not like the guys and their little girls who knew Wendell and Deanna from way back and drank cheap whiskey all night and fast, till Deanna ran out of bottles and had to pull the Jack down from the rail and sell it at well price. The difference was small sometimes and big other times, but everyone knew it, could see it, that gap between the hicks and the hippies. Between the people who knew the groove and the people who didn't know the groove, felt weird or iffy toward the groove maybe when they heard it, or were looking for something simpler than the groove, or were at least surprised and a little unhappy with themselves when they liked the groove.

It was already early June by then. The big-time heat was getting close, and we'd barely even had our usual two weeks of spring, when the leaves came back to the trees all at once and the woods got jungled. We'd had more storms than usual that spring—they'd blown through heavy and gray, the sky kind of rolling slowly down all day until it was night and so windy you couldn't light a smoke outside to save your life—so I was ready for summer, even if it was gonna be a rough one. A Friday, I think it was, because I remember Deanna complaining about having to run back to the storeroom for cases of Lone Stars and she only ever had to go that often when they were on twenty-five-cent special and that was Friday nights. It was the back half of the first set, and the room was fine but nowhere close to full, and we were playing some old stuff. Benny was sitting down at the piano, kind of wailing up at the top around a D-flat, and it was sounding good. Wendell had gotten it tuned that morning after all of Benny's nagging—some guy with a toolbox, and an ear, I guess, though he couldn't much play, had futzed around in it for an hour or two while I watched with a rip-roaring headache from a barstool—and I bet even Wendell felt good about it, even though the whole deal wasn't cheap, 'cause now the keys weren't clamming up or getting stuck, and the tuning was dead-on even in the high octaves. Everyone could tell. Benny'd wanted to try some Cash, so we did but dragged it out slow, and he let me really go in the bridge, and I stretched it out for two full minutes or so alone, and when I looked up from the solo and Hopper hit the downbeat, the crowd was pretty still. Even though I knew I'd gotten it, was totally on and sliding right. I should've known then there was something off about the room already. But instead we just kept moving. I'd been wanting to play "Thank God I'm a Country Boy" but keep it real minor and sad, so we did that too before we moved back into the normal stuff. We were fucking around a little bit, fine. It was absolutely fun as hell.

And I noticed down on the left side of the stage a boy grooving, a young kid with hair longer and even greasier than mine, and he was looking up at me with all this hope and excitement in his face, smiling and bobbing along with Hopper's floor tom, nodding his head real big. And not with anyone that I could clock, pretty surely alone. Once I saw the kid I really couldn't see anyone else in the crowd, and he was feeling it, really in it for the whole end of the set, and when we laid out the outro of "It's Gonna Be Easy," even though it was a little rocky and we had to build in an extra two measures to cut it off clean, he brightened so big it was hard to look at him, and he immediately came up to try to talk to Benny, but he was looking at me.

I propped my guitar against the wall and walked to the bar, through the people and the lights that Wendell had flicked back on, and Deanna handed me a beer by the neck with just her first two fingers, and I went out the side door for a break and a smoke. On my way toward the door, I noticed a group of guys, four or five of them, in their big boots and work jackets and close-cropped, army-looking haircuts, and they moved half aside for me to walk around them, but meanwhile they were all just kind of casually staring at the kid and at Benny and Hopper too and not talking much in a way that made me nervous. I went outside anyway. Smoked my cigarette and sat down on a low stack of pallets Wendell had pushed against the wall, thought about nothing much but listened to the noise inside and heard something high and trebly come on the box. I crushed the butt against the brick wall and breathed deep to try to get centered and on track for the second set, and that's where I was when I heard what sounded suddenly like too much movement inside. Like a real din, a loud party. It seemed wrong. I looked over at the door and saw one of the black chairs hit the doorway, like someone had tried to kind of fling the chair outside, but its legs caught and it clattered to the ground half-out and wrapped around the doorframe. I scrambled up. I had to step over it, or kind of leap a little awkward, to get back inside, and then I saw a big empty space in the middle of the floor, and Hopper had one of the hick boys in a headlock and was dragging him real rough out the front through a parting crowd of people.

33

Hopper was fucking strong, man, dragging that guy to the door like he was a kid even though he was probably six foot and a good 250. Hopper was not taking it easy. T.K. opened the door for Hopper and followed them both out. I saw Benny sitting down at a table against the wall with a hard face on, and the table was shaking 'cause he had his leg up against it jittering. It was really rocking.

I looked around the room for Wendell and found him standing by the bar, like he'd come out to do something but had gotten stuck over there, like his boots had gotten jammed in mud. He was standing still, he wasn't doing anything but watching, his eyes working back and forth between Hopper and the guy he was handling and the stage.

The poor kid who'd been so in the groove was beat half to hell, his eyes swelling up to his eyebrows already and one of his cheeks ripped open into a deep slit and bleeding a dark, almost-black sludgy blood, and he was propped up against the stage and alone but for Deanna, who was trying to sop up his face with a bar rag and her fingers. His face was pale, but so was the rest of him, and so I couldn't tell how much was from the licking and how much from just being that way. No one in Texas was pale like that. But he didn't look more than eighteen, if that. He had one of those faces that just keeps getting younger and younger the closer you look, so that if you get right up next to him you can see him so naive and gentle you kind of want to ruffle his hair or something. The rest of everyone didn't know what to do, it seemed like, and I felt a storm of eyes on my back. I moved toward the stage.

"The hell?" I asked. "What in the hell?"

"I don't know," Deanna said.

"What?" I asked again.

"Wendell was in the back, and I was covering, and everyone was at the bar. I didn't see much."

I looked at the kid. He was in bad shape and the room was dead quiet, like at some service, quieter than I'd ever heard it even including the first day I'd come in to test the sound, and now I knew everyone was looking over at us. Deanna was still wiping the kid's face in a circle but like she wasn't even focusing, so she was smearing the blood around more than cleaning it up. She was looking past me, around my side, and tilting her head, probably looking at Wendell. I squatted down in front of her and the kid so as to look into his eyes for a second, and when I did he said, "Beautiful music, man," and then swallowed a big hunk of spit. And then from behind me, clear as anything, I heard a deep voice say, "Faggot." I stood back up but didn't turn. I heard a table fall, and I knew it was Benny standing up.

"What the *fuck* is wrong with you, man," Benny said, but his face was red, and he sat back down in his chair with the table on the ground in front of him. I was still looking at the kid, and half waiting for Wendell to kick the guy out of the bar, but he didn't.

"Tell these boys this ain't California, or goddamn Mexico," that same voice said, but quieter, and then I could hear the front door swing open again, and he was gone.

I hoped Hopper was waiting.

The world felt pretty small then, and pretty sad. I tried not to move at all, even when the kid clenched his fists together on his lap and then let them fall back open, splay palms up on his lap. He had strangely beautiful fingers, could've played keys himself, but I knew somehow that he didn't. There was something in the way he'd watched us play that told me he'd never touched an instrument in all his life.

"What's your name, bud?" I asked, now standing straight up and looking down at him. His hair was blond and parted down the middle just like mine, and I could see a big seam of his scalp like an open road.

"Steven," he said. "I'm Steven."

"Cool, brother, very cool." I tried to keep my voice loud and normal, like the whole room wasn't looking at us. "Brother Steven," I said, "come outside for a smoke."

"Yessir, Mr. Moser, I'd be honored."

"Don't say that shit, Steven. It's ridiculous. My name's Doug."

"Yessir," he said again, and brushed Deanna's hand and the rag away from him like swatting a mosquito.

She pulled back, but she kept holding the rag out in front of her, away from her body. I turned around just as Wendell was starting to serve again and the place was calming down, and while the kid and I headed toward the back door, I took a quick glance around the room to see it starting to go back to normal. Still, there were a lot of boys who looked like they would've done or said the same fucking things as the guys Hopper'd gotten outside. It was kind of like they'd *all* done it anyway. I didn't know if Wendell was going to say anything at all. I heard a guy say jokey, "Fucking Christ, Wendell, whose bar *is* this?" and then I saw Deanna stand up and go back behind the bar, toward the kitchen, probably to wash her hands, still with the rag hanging out of one of them. Benny gave me a look like it'd been us who'd done something wrong, and then he looked back down at the floor. Me and the kid went out the side door. Hopper came around the corner of the building with T.K., who was flexing and rubbing a bruised hand, and those guys were gone.

But all through the second set the only thing I could think of when I was playing was Steven's fingers, long and delicate and shaking a little on his lap on the edge of the stage, like flipped-over insects on top of his jeans, and then outside, trying like hell to roll a smoke, long and delicate and womanly, really. Soft. And when I got back to the house that night, I went into the bedroom upstairs, the only other usable one, just to look at Jules for a second, and the next morning, I don't even know what I was doing, but I asked Gwen if she'd cut his hair. It was getting long.

It took me a day or two to feel all right again. I knew that even if Wendell tried to do something, the old boys would come back a couple nights later, once they'd cooled off and thought the place had too, but I didn't know about the kid Steven. He was a sweet kid, really. He dug, at least. He was too young though, maybe, to understand the thing about all of this—that these people didn't really know what we were doing with their music, fucking with it like we were, but they liked it, somehow they liked it. Of course they liked it. It was the only music with real soul they'd ever heard, and we busted the chords out and made them sound that way for a reason, and the reason was to get them to like it. The chords sustain and wander and resolve that way for a reason. But some of them didn't like the parts of themselves that liked it. God, and besides Hopper we were white boys anyway. What would they have done with the real shit? They got back in their cars and listened to John Denver on their radios and spit harder out the windows. They couldn't pin us down. We were the Lost Causes or the Good Goddamn or whatever Benny thought we should be called that week, but in the end we were more like them than they could handle, and we were from Texas, just down the goddamn road, and we were decent and kind after all, goddamn it, I swear we were. We just played them a little blues.

G wen had a chat with Wendell out on the porch before the place opened the next day—they got along pretty well, and he'd helped her with some house stuff I couldn't do. She had heard about the fight, if you'd call it a fight even, which I wouldn't, and was pissed I hadn't told her about it. She called my name a couple of times through the screen door, and I came outside even though I'd been in the middle of a new tune that sounded a little like "Dealer's Blues" but kept the progression straighter and cleaner, streamlined and with only one or two big, sharp slides.

If I took a second to notice, Gwen still looked as hot as she had when we got together. Back then I'd hang around wherever Powell and Lannie were playing. All the old bars up on the drag, and maybe most in the basement off Fourth underneath the warehouse. It'd gone through a bunch of names, but I always thought of it as just the Basement, and there was an old A-frame sign propped against the building that even read WELCOME TO THE BASEMENT real big and then smaller underneath it whoever was playing, but whoever had played a couple weeks ago usually—Ray never remembered to change it. Plus it was always the same guys anyway. Benny'd been coming in recently with his conjunto and mucking up the sound, and I loved it.

I saw Gwen on that street downtown for the first time, under a streetlight, and her hair was so long and that summer sort of red but piled up on her head, and she was wearing a skirt that kind of slipped down her hips a little too much and floated when she turned, more or less begging to be pulled off. She seemed to turn around a lot, spin almost. She pulled on her Slim, smiled her little-girl smile, ran her fingers down Joe's shirtsleeve. That was before I knew how smart she was, how sharp she could be—back when she'd still hide it in new company.

Out here on the porch it was hard to remember all that. Plus it was too early in the afternoon and Saturday even, and I'd put more coffee on but was waiting for the drip. I could see in the way her forehead crinkled up she had something on her mind and was going to tell me about it.

"Hey, were you going to tell me you got into a fight?"

"I didn't get into a fight, baby, where'd you hear that?" I said softly. My head was hurting. "You woulda known if I'd got in a fight."

"Wendell told me something happened last night."

"It wasn't a fight, and I was outside anyway. It was just some kids."

"It sounded like you were involved."

"He told you all this? Just came over and told you all this straight out?"

"What's so strange about that?" she asked.

I looked at her for a second.

"OK, no, not exactly. He just kind of mentioned it."

"I wasn't involved," I said, wiping a light sheen of sweat off my neck. "Hopper took care of it, but it really wasn't anything. Just some guys being assholes to a kid I didn't know."

I really wasn't involved. When had she gotten like this, so worried all the time about nothing? And bored with me too, somehow. I tried to count up the number of times she'd come over to see us play, and it was fewer than five, even though it was a forty-five-second walk across the parking lot. Her friends would come up weekend nights sometimes after Julian was in bed and sit on the porch, even, but they wouldn't walk across the damn lot.

"Why don't you come listen, baby? We've been trying some new stuff."

"I can hear it over here. With the doors open all the time? I can hear it."

She was wearing one of my old denim shirts over her T-shirt but unbuttoned, and she didn't have a bra on either, and I could see straight through it.

"It's a good room though," I said, looking at her. "You should come hear how it sounds."

"I know," she said, gentle. "Just please don't get into fights at the bar."

"I didn't get into a fight, Gwen. I really didn't."

"It's really not a lot to ask you to stay out of that shit, I don't think. Set an example, you know. Julian pays more attention than you think."

"Where's he at?" I wanted to be done with the conversa-

CALLIE COLLINS

tion before we got any deeper into it. I really didn't want to
start thinking about all the ways I was failing her—how old
I was getting and still doing the same damn thing, how little
I looked like a father, how I was too drunk the night before
to screw her when she'd waited up late for me, even. I knew
better than anybody how disappointing I could be.

"Julian? He's in the woods," she said. "Playing."

"Playing?" I asked, and she looked at me sideways but
didn't say anything at all. The porch was littered with the
little yellowed filters Gwen rolled into her cigarettes. They
were everywhere, all over the slats of the porch and down
through the spaces between them. There must be hundreds
under there already, I thought, and felt bad and trashy, litter-
ing this house that belonged to Deanna and Wendell, but the
feeling faded pretty quickly.

"What else is going on?" I asked.

"Not much." She spoke slow and looked at me real
intentionally.

"M'kay," I said. "Hey, I'll be right back."

I went inside, looked around for a minute, and realized
I was trying to see what was so great about the house that
was keeping Gwen from coming to the bar. I couldn't see
anything, really. We didn't even have a TV out here, not yet,
though I was meaning to get one for Jules as soon as I had
some extra cash. Gwen loved old westerns, though she'd get
embarrassed about it, Louis L'Amour and James Michener
and shit, which was notable for a girl like Gwen, because she
really was the smartest girl I'd ever known, and it charmed
me so much when I first saw the pile of them in her old

42

apartment on Speedway, back when she was still in school and walked around days with a pencil tucked behind her ear, that I thought I might keel over from love. I wanted to find that feeling again, but charm, the unexpected kind especially, isn't something you can just dredge up out of wanting. There were uneven stacks of paperbacks by the couch, a ragged copy of *The Second Sex* and a glossy hardback of *The Savage Mind*, and whatever she was in the middle of was flat open on the kitchen table. I didn't much understand what she could get out of reading obscure French shit or cowboy clichés that she couldn't get out of a good, stomping C-chord with a hammer on the seventh, but I guess I wouldn't know anyway.

I felt unsettled and empty. Gwen worked weekdays down at Dillard's now, in juniors, where she sold dresses to high school girls and had to plaster a fake smile on her face all damn day, which also meant a half-hour drive up to Hyde Park and another one to get back, and the truck's clutch was sticking, she told me. I hadn't driven it in a week or two even, I realized. I couldn't even remember the last time I'd been downtown. The days were blurring together, and most of what I knew about the time passing I knew by the way the air felt on my skin on the porch or in the lot or laying out where I'd taken to laying out—on the pallets on the side of the bar. I played and I drank and I slept and mostly I felt fine about it, but it occurred to me I could use some company besides Gwen and Jules and the guys and Deanna, when she'd stick around to talk for a minute. Some company I could choose. I'd been avoiding Wendell and I didn't even know why, but the day before I'd ducked into the bathroom between beers when I'd heard his boots crunching through the gravel outside the door and it was funny, I'd been thinking about Dee more than I'd really thought I had, and I wondered real fast what time it was and how long it'd be before she got up to the bar. The coffee was done, and I poured myself a cup and went back out onto the porch with these thoughts in my head.

"I gotta go see someone else play tomorrow, I think. I'll go down early and get somebody to take a look at the clutch if you want me to."

Gwen'd sat down on the top step, and while I was talking she laid full down on the porch rather than crane her neck back toward me.

"Wendell's gonna look at it. He said he would."

"Huh," I said. "Yeah?"

"He offered," she said.

I was quiet for a minute, and she looked at me.

"All right, then," I said. "I'm still going to go to the 'Dillo tomorrow."

"Did I ask you not to?" she asked, and then I saw her regret asking it the way she had. She looked at me with sorry in her eyes.

"Hey, Julian hasn't eaten yet. Want to go find him?" she asked.

I weaseled up to her. I traced a line with my finger along her jaw and under her chin, tried to lean over and kiss her, but my ribs got in the way, and she had to come up to meet me. She pulled away gently. I did love her so. She turned and put her cheek against my knee, grabbed her little smoke out of the slat where she'd jammed it, and pulled on it hard.

"You're gonna choke lying down like that." I took it from between her fingers, and she gave me her *don't fuck with me* look, but her eyes were smiling, and she lifted up and blew a big mouthful of smoke right into my face.

The drive down into town was pretty as hell, I'd always forget how pretty. The low ditches along 2244 were clotted with brush, but the road wound around small hills and limestone cliff walls that rose up suddenly and white as deer tails along the right-hand lane. The truck kind of floated down the center stripe, it felt like; I barely even had to steer it through the curves. Houses sat far off the road, down gravel driveways, and once every couple of minutes I'd pass a car sitting at the end of one and a person behind the wheel waiting for me to pass to pull out, and it would startle me, that was how alone on the road I felt. I had to hope I didn't hit anything, 'cause deer bolted fast out here and I'd had a couple beers already.

At the bottom of the biggest curve I passed the city limit sign and felt alive again, like I'd come out of hibernation, and I wanted to see people and hear Joe's voice do its growl on "Dallas" and smoke some so that I could really dance. I was running low up in the woods, and Gwen'd been smoking more than she used to, picking off leaves and spliffing her cigarettes, which was just a waste of good pot. You couldn't smoke pot with a filter, I kept telling her, what's the point? I crossed through the park and over the river and turned my head and got a good look at the water through the rusty slats of the low bridge. The surface rippled a little in the wind and ran dark green into the mouth of the city, and I gunned it, high on the town for a minute like I could get. Austin was a town you could get high on, easy. But then I couldn't upshift with the goddamn clutch the way it was and the truck stuttered under me, and suddenly it felt like my body was moving forward without it. I eased the brake under my foot, flexed my ankle in my boot. I came back down, annoyed and gloomy.

The Armadillo lot had no drainage, and half of it was one giant puddle from some old rain, so I nosed the truck alongside the edge of it, parked, and hopped out. The sun was setting and even in the reflection of the puddle, murky and dusty, it was beautiful, and so I looked up. Red and orange, and above it little spots of violet that looked darker than black. I wanted to hold it somehow, to keep it with me awhile, but then I felt hopeless, a half-wit for wanting that. I headed through the gate in the fence toward the beer garden. They'd painted this horse mural up on the wall, and the horse was bucking and the rider on it was smiling and kind of leering down at the gate, watching people walk in and out, and it made me laugh every time I saw some girl come out underneath it. A group of four of them passed me and smiled and opened their bodies up toward me when I walked past them.

In the garden people sat at the long picnic tables and held

their cups of Shiner with both hands. I got in line to get myself a beer, hoping that by the time I made it up to the bar, Phil would get back from wherever he was so I wouldn't have to pay for it. I couldn't remember the last time I paid for a drink, I realized. I wasn't about to start now, I was thinking, and then Phil appeared right on cue. He said hey, pumped the keg under the bar with his right arm, one-two-three, floated the foam, and it was like I'd been around as much as I had in the winter, in December and January, and it felt like I'd never moved up to the woods at all. I saw some girls I knew a little bit from their hanging around Joe, and one of them had been hanging out with Benny for a while, though not so long I could remember her name, but I needled in and sat down with them anyway. One of the girls was rolling and offered me a smoke, and I took it from her and tucked it behind my ear until she had hers all rolled and we could light them together.

"Where y'all been?" asked the one I knew from Benny. "I heard you were playing somewhere new."

"A honky-tonk," said one of the other ones. "You getting back to your roots? Or somebody else's roots?"

I smiled. "They're all honky-tonks," I said.

"Nah, they're not," a different one said. "Look at us, do we look like we're at a honky-tonk?"

And I did, I looked at them. They were all pretty like birds, skinny skinny, with little sharp faces and sweaty, their shirts drooping real hot from their tits.

"Y'all should come up," I said, and the cigarette girl laid her Zippo flat inside my palm and kind of brushed my fingers on her way out. "We got a crowd out there, and there's a real good dance floor."

"Too damn far," a voice said coming up behind me, and Joe flicked my collar up with two fingers. "No one wants to drive halfway to Kerrville to see you play, Dougie, you're not *that* good. Maybe if it was me." He came around the end of the table and leaned one hand against it and smiled at me. "You can't even come down anymore?"

"I'm here now, ain't I?" I asked, and I knew he wasn't really mad, couldn't care less if I was there as long as the girls were and the amps were up loud and people were grooving. Hell, I was happy he'd noticed.

"Where's Gwen?"

"At home with Jules," I said.

"How you got that girl to have your kid I'll never know," he said. "How's it up there anyway?"

"It's damn good," I said. "Actually, the sound's great."

"Glad to hear it, then. I gotta get there," he said. "Sooner, maybe, if you'd get up tonight and play Sandy's Gibson for a couple minutes?"

"Hell yes I will," I said so fast and sure that I surprised even myself.

The girls were talking about something else, but I felt a little squeeze and noticed that the one who'd rolled me the cigarette had her hand tucked in around my left elbow.

"Good deal, bub, glad to hear it." Joe smiled. "I gotta check now, but come test it out in a while before we go on," he said. "It's sounding real good and pure tonight, and it's holding the tune, Sandy restrung it." He took a drag of his

49

smoke and then clenched his teeth down on it and smiled around it the way he did, and he looked kind of like a clown, and I was proud to know him and laughed. He went back inside and left me there at the table. The girl scooted over so I could feel her thigh underneath her thin skirt pressing up against mine, and I drank some of my beer, pretended to listen to their talk but nah, lost the thread eventually, and spent a couple of minutes looking around the garden instead.

I felt at home at the Armadillo, more than I did at Rush Creek, even though I was spending all my damn time there and was already used to it. Here it just smelled like home without trying, like dirt and sweet beer spilled all over and skunk, and the buzz of everyone's voices and the cars pulling into the lot and their doors slamming and the kick drum beating through the doors during check made me feel as warm as mid-August, surrounded by love and the goodness of the universe, like I was the best version of myself I could be. I'd been sleeping too much, so much my dreams had gotten crazy, and while I sat there feeling the air and the kindness with my eyes closed or half-closed and the girl's hand on my shirt and the metal of her bracelet pressing into my forearm, a flash of one of the dreams came back to me, and I tried to hold it down and trace it for a minute, something about Gwen or my father, whom I hadn't called in too long and was living alone now in Brenham, and I worried about him when I thought about him, so I tried not to, and plus Danny was down there, just down the street, in case anything happened.

But no, the dream was about Deanna, wasn't it, after all? A big feeling of déjà vu took my brain over, and I could see Deanna sneaking into my house to play my guitar, and in the dream I hadn't been surprised, not at all, I'd just watched her thinking she was alone from the doorway of the bedroom. And when I finally came back down to earth, to the beer garden, and opened my eyes wide, the sun was gone completely and the lights were blinking on one bulb at a time and everyone was all lit up and the sweet girl's hand still in the crook of my arm, and I could see then, through and over people's shoulders, that that kid Steven was coming toward me. I straightened my face out into a normal shape and stood up to say hello.

S teven wouldn't leave me alone all night, not all night, and all the way through the opener he stood next to me, way too close. The gash on his cheek was starting to scab over yellow, and his eyes were so sunken inside their bruises I could barely make them out. A little metal cross hanging at his collarbone I hadn't noticed before, like that was gonna do anything for him. His breath smelled like rot, which I knew because he kept leaning over to say things to me about the tunes while the band was still in the middle of playing them, and I tried to ignore him, but that just seemed to make him want to talk to me more, so I tried the only other thing I could think of, which was to drink so fast I could keep him going off for more beers over and over, and that way I could be rid of him and listen to the music the way I wanted to for at least a minute or two. Boy, I chugged, I was chugging. I'd lost track of the girl, but I was sure I'd find her a little later when I wanted to and hoped faintly that she'd be as drunk or stoned as I was bound to be, slamming Shiners like this. I felt a little bad about making the kid spend so much cash on me, but then he came back with round five or six and was rushing to get to where I was standing in the back of the crowd so fast he had a hard time coming to a stop and spilled the foam off one of the beers onto my boot and all over the carpet too.

"Sorry, brother." He leaned over and smiled real big. "You can have the other one."

I nodded slowly and kind of solemn, in a way I thought would say to him *Fine*, but to pay me back for the fact that my boots were gonna smell like rank beer for days, *Please, dear God, shut up for half a minute*, and I turned my head back toward the stage.

"I'm clumsy, I've always been clumsy, that's why I can't play even though I'd wanna play like you do," he said, his words hot and said so close to me it made me nervous.

I nodded without even inclining my head toward him.

"You know?" he said.

"Yeah," I mouthed, still facing the band.

"Wish I could play," he said. "I'd probably be best at keys if I could hold still, 'cause I got big hands, I know, but the way you play the guitar, Doug, I'm just so jealous of it. Nah, never mind, envious, I'm envious of it. You know the difference?"

I nodded again, this time just a single dip of my head. It was never-ending. The opener finished out the set with a good cover of "Dallas," which was risky 'cause "Dallas" was hard without a real good piano, but there was a guy up there playing the trumpet real warm and slow, and it sounded goddamn sexy like that, and I wondered what Joe thought of what they were doing with his tune. I looked at the trumpet player. He'd moved over from pedal steel, which was hilarious, really made me laugh, 'cause he was playing both so well.

Benny would've loved it, and I wished he was in the room to hear it pump, but I hadn't seen him. We weren't the only guys pulling horns or accordion into our sound anymore, or playing with the idea at least.

"Hoo boy, that sounds *good*," Steven yelled over a big blast of the horn, and I hated him, fast and sudden, for ruining this for me. I wasn't the fighting type, never had been, but I felt the urge to hit him and realized quick that most people probably had that urge with this kid, that I'd probably seen only one of the many beatings he'd gotten in his life, and he was still real young. I clenched the hand that was farther away from him and then tried to focus on letting my fingers relax one by one out of the fist. He was still talking, but the music did sound good, and I tried to direct all my energy toward it instead of him. By the time the song ended I felt calmer, even made myself turn to him and say, "Yeah yeah," before we walked outside to smoke while the crew broke down and set back up for Joe's set.

Outside I found that girl—Janet, I asked—or she found me was more like it, and she rolled me another cigarette, real quick and tight. She was a pro at it. I leaned against the edge of one of the picnic tables and smoked it. I was approaching drunk, man. My feet were sweating. And she was getting up real close to me, but Steven was still there and looking at us like a dog or something, jealous, or envious or whatever. *What the hell is the difference anyway?* I thought, but I sure didn't want to ask and get him going. Anyway, she said she had to go visit the ladies' room and drilled me point-blank in the eyes with her own, and so I said I'd go inside with her, and I did actually need to piss, and I asked Steven if he'd stay and save the end of the table so we wouldn't lose our seats, made it sound as much as I could like he was doing me a big favor, was my man for the job, and then I followed Janet in through the door into the room and then back out the front and around the dark side of the building, where she pulled me up against the wall and pushed her tongue real gently between my lips and used it somehow to cup mine. And sure, I'm never proud of it, but boy that girl was hot and had one hand sliding up my back under my shirt and the other in my hair, and I was getting too into it too fast, because of the beers and the relief too of escaping the kid and just how happy I was to be at the Armadillo. Anyway I thought she was about to let me pull her skirt up right there on the side of the building, but I heard the crunch of somebody's boots and I pulled away real fast and kind of crossed my legs, awkward but best I could, but Joe didn't even come around the corner, just said, "Dougie, let's go, brother, get it later." I was annoyed, but the girl laughed, and I kissed her neck real fast and remembered suddenly I had to piss anyway, and I told him I had to use the bathroom real quick but I'd meet him by the stage, and he said sure, he bet I did, and I said I'd be in in a minute.

The walk to the bathroom was rough, I was sliding a little from all the beers, but I stood in front of the sink trough for a minute and looked myself real deep in the eyes and splashed some water on my face even though the water in the men's reeked of sulfur all the time, there was some kind of leak they couldn't fix, and so I felt fine and straighter once I got to the little stairs beside the stage, where Sandy was pissed and yelling at Joe. Joe'd decided he wanted me to play the whole set on Sandy's Gibson, with its new strings and everything, and Sandy was real riled up about it, but it was Joe's call, always Joe's call. Steven was suddenly right beside me as if he'd fucking zapped in from the garden or something, and he handed me a fresh beer. I squeezed the plastic cup, and it puckered in around my thumb and fingers, and I took a slow drink, thinking that Joe better let me play the whole set or I'd have to listen to this goddamn kid talk through the whole thing and want to kill him all over. I was a nice guy—I worked real hard to be a nice guy—and feeling that angry at somebody I barely knew made all the acid churn up in my stomach. And anyway, Sandy took a fast look at me like he'd found me with his sister and slapped the wall as he walked away. Steven tapped my shoulder and said, "Hey, Doug, man," like he needed something, but I made like I didn't hear him, and the lights went down and then, thank God, we were on.

N ow, I used to play country music when I was young, sure, real deep-classic country. I mean, we all did, didn't we? That old Lefty Frizzell twang and my mama waltzing with the sink to "I Can't Help It (If I'm Still in Love with You)." And I still did love the acoustic, fooling around with the true blue chords, the big jangly major chords without hammers or pull-offs or slides at all, just a G into a full C into a little sustained D and coming back down to the G. Strumming clean and only on the downbeats. You didn't even need your fingers for it or barely, 'cause it wasn't nothing, country music. I did still love it some. Lord, I grew up on that shit. And anyway, it had led me to now, so I don't fault it, though when I hear it on jukes and even some of the shit they play in the early-afternoon shows on KOKE, I do wonder how boys can still be kicking that can around without listening to Freddie King or Albert Collins and letting it dirty them up at least a little, and then I remember where I am: in Texas still. In Texas.

And up there onstage with Joe I couldn't remember myself how I'd ever been happy with something so *old*. The blues was new all the time, man, it had to be new all the time. Sandy's Gibson sounded like honey, and it flowed and dripped like honey, and I couldn't stay in one chord for more than two bars without feeling like the guitar was just gonna go on and move without me. I was drunk all right, but the guitar was just as drunk as I was, it seemed, and when we finished up "Saturday Night," and Joe screamed over the crowd at me that we could play anything, whatever I wanted to play, I walked over to him and asked loud in his ear if he knew this old Bill Monroe bluegrass song it had occurred to me it'd be fun to mess with.

"Fuck you, brilliant, of course," he said, and did a little tap on the stage with his foot and took the three steps back to Geoff on the drums, and Geoff screamed out, " 'Walk Softly on This Heart of Mine,' " to the guys, and Jimmy cracked his neck and lifted up the horn to his lips, and Geoff yelled, "I'll go with the kick, wait for it," and then hit the kick four beats and Joe sang real close and intimate into the mic— "*You say you're sorry once again, deeeeeeeear*"—and the chords dropped, and we tucked in. It was so good and sure that halfway through the second chorus I held the Gibson up away from my body and kind of folded my legs underneath me and sat down on the stage so I could bend over the guitar, have it closer to me, really up against my chest, while I grooved. I was so in it I barely even noticed I was sitting down, and I wouldn't even remember it at all, except that I was still sitting there when Joe let the horns solo and I looked up from the guitar and the crusty carpet around me into the crowd and saw Wendell's face looking right at me.

I didn't even really think *Shit* at first. I just thought, *Oh, there's Wendell over there,* and it took probably ten seconds of skating around the D, falling into the flat, when it occurred to me looking down at the beautiful shiny gold of the Gibson that I'd done something wrong, or was in the middle of doing something wrong. But it didn't feel wrong. The Gibson was hot butter, and I resented Wendell real fast and hard for making me feel guilty, for making me feel anything other than the music and how I was meant to play it, and all of this while I was still soloing just how I'd wanted, so I was in between feeling the heavenly floating feeling I get when I really pull on a note as far as it can go—how it hovers there on the edge of the sharp like a little rock on a ledge or something quivering, totally in control—and a feeling of shame, which is, bar none, the worst feeling of them all.

Jesus, why was everyone trying to ruin my good night? Plus I was still real blitzed. In fact I had to check a couple of times, look up like I was just grooving with the crowd and try to focus my eyes to make sure it really was Wendell standing there. But goddamn yes, it was. He was unmistakable even though in my head he looked like he was swimming around, swimming and bobbing in a big pool of people with his head a full foot above the rest. The song ended and I stood up, but I realized I couldn't leave Joe high and dry up there onstage and I didn't know where Sandy was anyway.

Joe pointed at me while the keys warmed up behind me for the next song, and he said, "Doug Moser, baby," and the crowd yelled out real loud.

I was happy, truly happy, until I realized I was going to

have to stay up there and play the rest of the set with Wendell watching me. It wasn't going to be pretty, and I was going to have to keep the Gibson as toned-down as I could, I thought, to be respectful, but I really hated being respectful when I felt like I had to, so fuck it, I said to myself, and I played as well as I ever played for the next thirty minutes, forty-five even. When the last song finally ended, we came down the side steps and I tried to follow Joe into the room to wait out for the encore, but I wavered slightly and felt a hand clap down hard on my shoulder like the hand of God or something, and I knew I was going to have to have a conversation. But when I turned around and looked up for Wendell's face, I was looking at the ceiling. It'd been Steven who'd clapped me.

"Dougie, man, can I just tell you," he started, while I scanned out over his shoulder.

I sorted through the heads in the first couple rows as quick as I could, which wasn't very. My head was pounding from the noise and the beers, and the faces were kind of strobing and not staying real still, but I didn't see Wendell. He wasn't where he'd been standing. People were shouting over one another and someone on the PA said "JOE ELY" real big, and a couple sweet girls grouped together and talking to each other in the front turned their heads back toward the stage. Joe and the guys came out of the room behind me.

Steven was still talking, saying, "Just wild, brother, you were so deep I couldn't barely even see you."

I looked for Wendell but couldn't find him, and I knew

in my heart he'd walked out the door the moment we ended the set.

"You were just *music*," the kid said, "like God was making it," and I don't even know why but I looked him in the eyes and then I had the urge to spit real ugly at his feet. I could almost see myself doing it too, could imagine a long thread of spit hanging down near his shoe, and me wiping my mouth with the sleeve of my shirt. But of course I didn't, and he was still talking, and I couldn't look him in the eyes anymore. I climbed the steps without saying anything, got back on the stage with the neck of the Gibson still tight in my fist, like a little thing I was choking. Still, I felt all right. I played the whole encore, and the room knew the songs and they knew Joe and they knew me, and I felt a lot of love swirling around with the notes. It's only now, when I look back on it, that it seems like that night at the Armadillo was when things really started to go bad, to just spoil and sour the way good things sometimes do.

The days after that were bad, flat-out bad. I felt the kind of bad you can't escape from, like it's in the air somehow and sticky, so that it's the first thing you feel coming down on you when you wake up and the last thing you feel, and all over your skin, when you're trying to quiet your whole body down and get some sleep.

The morning after I played that set with Joe was bound to be ugly anyway, 'cause I was hungover as all hell and it was one of the bad ones. I had the anxious bout real early in the morning, four or five, still dark. I was too hungover to even sleep, was instead just lying in bed, and Gwen had pulled the sheet all the way over to her side and was wrapped in it, so I was prickling and dripping under the quilt her mama'd given us after we came back from Houston and told them we'd gotten hitched, this wool thing, and I was really itching. Gwen was dead asleep, and I'd thanked God for that when I'd come in but now it felt lonely and I wished I had her there to talk to. But I couldn't bring myself to wake her up either. I must've stayed still like that all the way through the sun rising until the alarm went off, and then I closed my eyes and pretended to be out while Gwen got up and dressed and Jules did his running all over the house and she left to drop him at a friend's house and go down to Dillard's for the day. I let her leave without even opening my eyes. I got up eventually to make myself a pot of coffee, but I was so out of it and jittery that I dumped too much coffee in the filter all at once and it caved in and sank down into the middle, and then when I tried to fish it out I spilled grounds all over the kitchen, the counter, and the floor. My hands shook when I tried to pull another filter off the others in the pack.

I must've had a lot—those mornings happen when I've had so much that my blood can't run it out by the morning—and I'm not a lightweight, let's put it like that, and I'd been drinking cheap beer too. Yeah, some whiskey in the garden after the set, and then Joe'd had a baggie of something, which helped then but wasn't helping now. A lot of the night was blurring together, but I remembered, standing there in the kitchen, waiting for the water to boil, how good it'd sounded in the room, how in the middle of a song I'd looked up from the guitar and seen the energy I can sometimes see, like crackling golden strings in the air and a true connection between people, and I was trying to remember that soft feeling and bring it back into my body somehow when I heard a little knock at the door and saw Deanna through the window, standing there in a big work shirt and acting like she couldn't see straight through into the kitchen where I was standing. I looked down and saw I was just in my underwear.

"Hang on," I said as kindly as I could, which wasn't very, or didn't sound kind anyway, and then I beat myself up a little for snapping at her accidentally while I ducked into the bedroom and turned my jeans right side out and pulled them on. I got on a T-shirt and closed my eyes and pushed my fingers real hard into my temples, held them there for one-two-three-four, and then went back out and opened the door.

"Hey, Dee," I said, and came out onto the porch.

"Well, shit, I know that look when I see it," she said.

She pulled back a little bit as I walked a big arc around her and pulled my cigarettes out of my pocket, like she didn't want to be nearer me than she had to. I offered her one.

"Thanks," she said, and took it out of my hand with two long fingers. There was a box of matches sitting on the porch rail, and I grabbed them and tried to scratch one out, but the box was wet and so were the matches. I could barely hold my palm flat. Deanna pulled a lighter out of the pocket of her jeans, lit hers, and handed it to me. We stood there like that for a second, and I looked down and noticed my shirt was somehow inside out and backward, so the tag was right under my damn neck. I pulled at the collar.

"How you doing?" she asked.

"Oh, I'm doing all right, I'm all right," I said. "Good."

"Yeah?" she asked.

"Went down to town last night for a couple of drinks and had one too many, I think, but I'll be right in an hour or two. Needed this too," I said, and held up my cigarette like it was saving my ass somehow. If anything I felt worse.

"I've got some Tylenol over there in the bar if you need it," she said.

"Y'all are up here early," I said. I didn't usually see her

or Wendell before two or three, when one or both of them showed up to start opening the joint. She had this old little Mazda I liked, and she pulled it into the lot real slow so as to not get gravel flying and scrape it up, which was sweet exactly the way she was sweet.

"It's just me," she said.

"Ah, OK."

"You want me to grab the Tylenol for you? It'd help."

"Nah," I said. "This smoke and some coffee'll do the trick. You want some? Coffee? Just made a pot."

"No, thanks," she said.

"OK."

"Thanks though," she said, and looked at me. It was a little cooler out than it'd been in a while actually, and she was using her nonsmoking hand to hold her shirt closed over her tank top. The sky was blue, the kind of blue that mocks you a little for feeling like such shit, for being such shit you can't even really see it.

We stood there for a minute just smoking.

"Gwen's at work?" she asked out of the silence, and even in my state I thought I heard a little edge in the question, a little opening, and I let myself think maybe she was asking something else.

"Yeah," I said, and shifted my weight onto my heels, "she'll be there all day."

"Oh," Deanna said with no wanting in her voice at all, not that I could hear, and she finished her cigarette, held the butt up to me like I might want her to put it somewhere, and I looked around for something that could be an ashtray, like we'd been using one out here the whole damn time, and I grabbed an old Coke can sitting at the foot of one of the chairs and offered it to her. She squeezed the butt in and turned like she was going down the stairs, but before she did she looked at my feet and said, "He's not exactly happy, Doug."

"Huh?"

"He's not in a good mood about the Armadillo last night. Wendell. I know it seems small."

I didn't say anything, but I felt real silly all of a sudden, like there was any chance in hell she was going to come over here and ask where Gwen was and come with me into the house with her jeans and her hair down and let me get up to something. And the feeling silly got me annoyed. And my head hurt, and still I didn't say anything.

"He's not petty, really, I'm just telling you so you know," she said.

"I dunno what in the hell you're talking about," I said, and tried to be slow about it, felt bad for the *hell* as soon as I'd said it. The whole night was coming back to me like it'd happened to somebody else, seeing Wendell so tall and weird-looking, standing out there in the crowd on the floor, and then spilling my guts out in the garden about how truly tiny and shitty it was that Wendell was going to be pissed about it when it was just music anyway and playing at the Armadillo would probably be *good* for all of us, better than anything Wendell could do to get folks to drive up here. I was ranting and being messed up and uncool about it like I hate doing, and to that goddamn kid Steven, after I'd looked all around

66

for that cigarette girl and couldn't find her and had to drive him home instead. I remembered flashes of the ride south, a blinking streetlight through the window, and then his house and trying to get him out of the truck. How'd I even gotten back here? Jesus.

"Don't do that, Doug," Deanna said. "Please. It's a small town, and he said you saw him anyway."

"Where?" I asked, and I reached for another cigarette.

"The Armadillo," she said, and looked at me like I'd be disappointing her if I tried to flat deny it. "All right, please just—" she started, but she walked down the steps without finishing it, without telling me what to do, and she sounded ashamed of me, which made my chest feel caught like in a trap.

"Deanna," I said.

"OK," she said back, kindly, but she was already walking across the lot toward the bar and pulling her keys out of her pocket.

Thank Christ we didn't have to play that night. Mondays weren't ever worth it, we'd all kind of decided together. I was way too hung-up and jonesy to play well, so I was glad for the day. But I got it in my head that I needed to go over there anyway, hair-of-the-dog it, and see if I could get a sense of whether I'd really have to do anything about this Wendell business. So I tried to close my eyes for a couple hours, ate some meat off a chicken Gwen had in the fridge with some real dry bread and a beer or two, and wandered over around five or five thirty to sit at the bar. I felt useless in the house alone; I could never really get myself comfortable in private unless I was playing, and I didn't want to play. I needed the noises and the smells and the sounds to feel like I was worth anything without a guitar in my hands. It occurred to me that there was another advantage of the bar being right here, and if I wanted to sneak over and spin the janky little lock on the back door I could have the bar all to myself whenever I wanted. Shit though, I almost fell over getting myself across the lot.

Dee was wiping down a couple of tables, and there was

a group of boys in the corner, young, maybe eighteen, nine-teen, but in work clothes, and I could smell them across the room, leather and onions, and they were being mostly quiet, flipping quarters occasionally. Nobody was behind the bar, and I didn't hear the sink or the washer running in the back, which meant Wendell wasn't there, or at least not yet, which was fine with me. What I really wanted was to talk to Deanna some more, see if I could get a handle on the feel-ing between us and fix it if I could. I'd been thinking about her all afternoon, and it felt good to think about her unless I remembered her sad voice floating up back toward me on the porch, so I tried to put that out of my mind and pretend like instead she'd come in the house, even though I knew that she probably never would've done that, even if I'd said exactly the right thing and it wasn't the morning after I'd gone around on my deal with Wendell. She came over to pour me the few fingers of good whiskey I asked for, like I needed when I was hanged like this, and tossed me a fresh matchbook from a box on the shelf above the mirror, but then she disappeared again, busied herself with things that didn't seem to even need doing, and only came back around to grab longnecks when the guys in the corner yelled her down.

I wanted to talk to her, I really did. I still felt kind of weak, but the pours were helping, and I thought about how to call her over and get her to sit with me for a while. I readjusted on the leather of the stool, stretched my legs straight under the bar. "Hey, Deanna," I said, next time she came near.

"You need something?"

"I was just gonna ask you. Thought if you could use some

69

help," but I couldn't think of how in hell I could help. There wasn't anything to do on Monday nights.

"You're sweet," she said. She looked at me hard then, like wondering if what she'd said was true.

I couldn't tell what she decided.

"The house still treating y'all good?"

"It's something else," I said. "So big we could spend every day in a different room."

She smiled. I'd never really asked too much about the house. I had this weird idea that I could jinx it, like if I talked too much about living there for free, they'd change their minds.

"Do you know about it? I mean, how long it's been there? Gwen said she thought it'd been a long time since anybody'd lived in it," I said, but then I realized that was probably a rude thing to say.

But Deanna leaned up against the bar, crossed one ankle behind the other, and resettled like she was gonna stay for a while.

"I know exactly how long it's been there," she said.

"Ah," I said. We were both quiet, and I didn't know why.

"You know," Deanna said. "You don't know Wendell very well yet, but he's a good man, even when he doesn't know how to show it. I hate it when he's upset."

I wondered if Gwen would say that about me, *I hate it when he's upset.* I wondered if Gwen could even tell when I *was* upset. I wondered if Gwen knew I was upset all the goddamn time.

"Sure," I said.

"I mean it," she said, but soft. "You remind me of him sometimes. How he was when he was younger."

"I do?"

She shifted on her feet, grabbed a real old unlabeled green bottle I'd never seen before out from the rail, and a new glass for me too. She poured something clear; it looked homemade. "It's one of those old Sears kit houses," she said. "My father built it."

"Your dad?" I was genuinely pretty surprised. I didn't know Deanna was from here. Really from here? Austin wasn't a place anybody was really from anymore, not these days, at least not a place anybody's whole family was from. Nobody I knew'd been here before about '60, '65.

"A Magnolia. That's what the model's called. They stopped making them 'cause nobody wanted the big colonials anymore after the forties."

"He built the whole thing by himself?"

"Well," she said, and made a noise with her tongue. "He shouldn't have. But you know, he just ordered it and they sent him the pieces on a truck. Cut the wood for him and everything. Still, it didn't look anything like the pictures when he was done with it."

I got a brief flash of her father, a guy who ordered a house like that out of a damn catalog. I thought I might write him into a song. I didn't see much. A blurry face.

"This is, uh," I said, holding up the glass to my eye. "Wow."

She nodded like she was proud, but I got the sense suddenly that even though she'd volunteered all that information, I was running out of time to ask questions. "Y'all never lived in it?" I asked.

"No, we didn't," she said. "We thought we might eventually, and Wendell fixed it up as best he could right before that big storm in 'sixty-eight, but then it took out the windows so he had to do it all over."

"Damn."

"Well, I did, I guess," she said. "When I was a girl."

"What?"

"I lived there as a kid. But I don't have a lot of fondness for it. It never really much felt like mine."

"Right," I said. I looked at her.

"Dee," I started, but then I got embarrassed. I could feel the old liquor bubbling up with the new liquor in my system, and I had to take a big swallow to push it back down. "I'm real sorry," I said.

"I know," she said, gentle. It felt like she was telling me the truth.

Me and the guys got back on the stage that week and I had a little talk with them to see if we could try out some new songs, try some jumpier stuff, 'cause I was already getting bored out here in the woods with the same old shit and it made me think probably the crowd was too. I don't think I really thought the crowd was bored. I was just talking. It was mostly for me, so I could get back to that feeling I'd had playing on the floor at the 'Dillo during "Walk Softly," and maybe a little bit 'cause the crowds were getting bigger, they really were and I was feeling it. I started to notice. I wanted to show people what we could do.

And the thing that was happening was that after Joe came up that Tuesday—walked in an hour before the first set even and with a big group of folks and more climbing out of cars in the lot, greeted me with a smack on the ribs and Benny with a beer Joe said he owed him for being just so goddamn pretty—was that the crowds at Rush Creek were becoming our crowds, our people. Girls I knew from Donn's and the Armadillo, Benny's old buddies from when he used to work the grill at Nau's, and even some of Gwen's friends dropped by before they headed over to the house to see the first couple songs. I turned around one night between sets and saw Gwen by the door, talking to T.K. I hadn't seen her in the bar in what felt like months. She looked proud of me, put her hand on my chest when I came over to say hey and said, "Aren't they sounding killer?" to her friends like she was telling and not asking, and I smiled wide and so did she. I never had really liked her friends, and they didn't like me either—they'd blamed me when she'd dropped out of school—but it was fine really, having them there. At least it was better than most nights, knowing there was a whole crowd of girls in the house when they could have been dancing with us instead. Deanna was slammed behind the bar, rushing around trying to pour, and Wendell hauled bags of ice in from the back to fill the beer troughs.

Wendell hadn't said anything to me about any of it, about the Armadillo or the crowds getting bigger, but I could feel his attitude shift the room around when Joe came in, and I was angry about it. My playing that Gibson had gotten him customers, which was what he'd hired us for, all he'd brought me and the guys up here for, and still I could tell he wasn't over it from the way he was avoiding me, looking over my shoulder when he talked to me, which he wasn't doing much anyway. I started to notice new things about Wendell, 'cause I was paying so much attention to him and how he was treating me all cold, and, to be honest, that week I started to get to disliking Wendell a little bit. But it wasn't even the way he was ignoring me or us, totally disappearing when Hopper broke a cymbal clamp and needed Wendell to unlock the closet in the back, or slamming beers down on the bar so hard it was making the girls jump and look down at the floor. It was that he wasn't talking much to Deanna either, and it was Dee who'd let it slip later that week, Thursday night, after most everyone was gone and the jukebox was rolling with Willie's new record, in that real quiet stretch at the end of the night and my ears still buzzing a little from the big slam of "Blackjack" and the scream of the bar after it, that Wendell had gotten pretty mean at some guy in line with him at the Kash-Karry and had gotten asked to leave without his groceries. She said it casual, but I knew it wasn't casual by how hard she was working to make it sound so. She didn't sound pissed at me, didn't tell me like it was anybody's fault and surely not mine. Still, it had been only a couple days since the 'Dillo, so it felt like it was.

Wendell came out from the back to fold and stack chairs, and I watched him from my stool. He moved around the folks who were still drinking at the tables but not very grace-fully, I mean, he was never graceful. He was a lunk, truly, I could see it so clearly from where I was. Hopper and Benny said hello when he came close to where they were sitting in a booth with some guys, a friend of Benny's down from Fort Worth and a couple of girls, and when Wendell looked over, he stood there too long kind of staring at Benny and his friend. Benny'd gone back to looking at one of the girls, but Wendell stood there kind of locked, and I watched him seeing these people different, seeing us different, and not lik-ing what he saw, not wanting us in the bar and regretting having given us the gig. It was a split second, but I saw it in the way he stood there. Wendell went back to what he was doing, snapped a chair folded with one hand and added it to the stack against the wall.

"I'm closing up, y'all," he said to no one directly but kind of to the whole room, and Hopper yelled back, "Ten-four," and everyone stayed where they were. Willie was still playing on the box, "Red Headed Stranger." I shot back the last dregs of my drink and lit a cigarette for the walk across the lot and yelled bye to Deanna through the kitchen door. I couldn't be in the room anymore with Wendell acting like he was, and it was only, what? Thursday. We were on for the next three nights in a row.

76

Yeah, and after the night at the Armadillo, the fucking kid was suddenly around the whole time. All the time. Suddenly it seemed like I couldn't escape Steven and his blond shag and his too-sweet-smelling Parliaments and his attention, his constantly bringing me drinks when I hadn't even asked for them, and the way he moved around Rush Creek like he suddenly felt like he owned part of it. Didn't he remember getting his ass kicked? Those guys were still here. They were everywhere, those same guys, coming around to see Wendell and drink and scratch stupid shit into the stall door in the bathroom. Mean shit. They watched us play and the crowd dance from the booths lined up by the front door, and I kept thinking they were going to get sick of it and stop coming around, but they didn't, there were still at least two dozen of them on busy nights, slamming Lone Stars in the back and flicking the caps at people. The other night one of them had gotten up in the middle of "Tomorrow" and gone up to the bar and started talking to Wendell, but as loud as he could, so loud the whole bar could hear his voice between the

77

guitar and the piano, and he was monologuing, really going for it, just to ruin the music, I thought.

Benny let his guitar slip off his knee. I stopped too.

"Hey, pal," Benny said into his mic.

Tulsa was sitting in on bass, and he stopped mid-line. I knew Hopper had his teeth gritted back there like he could chew right through a rock.

"Friend," Benny said. "You see this?" He held up his Fender. "Shut your fucking face," he said, and hey, lemme tell you, the guy looked surprised. I could see him glare up at Benny, but nobody said anything and with the whole bar quiet like that, yeah, he shut his face. Benny grinned and launched back in, and it felt good. Like we'd won one.

It was the way Steven moved. He was a nice kid, he really was, but he moved like a bird. Too gentle and close and sometimes he'd flutter somehow, so fast it could make you sick. Too nice too, really. What he would do is get up right at the front of the crowd, right at the edge of the stage, and he would close his eyes and he would groove, but he'd put his beer down on the floor and groove with his whole body, kind of sway and shake with the rhythm of the guitar, and when I'd bend the notes real wide, he'd bend his knees and roll with them. The kid was into the blues, but even the people who were coming up from town, even the hippest of the kids, couldn't bring themselves to stand near Steven while he was grooving. There's feeling the music, and then there's embarrassing, and the kid was embarrassing himself. And he was embarrassing me too most of the time, to be honest. But I can't say it didn't sometimes feel good to look out through the new lights Wendell'd rigged up and see the music just moving him wherever it wanted to. When it felt real good up there, I could look out and see Steven, and it was like my notes were coming into him and out of him, like there was no boundary between the sound and his body. It was weird and I couldn't look too long or I'd get all red and tight, but it felt special too, to make somebody move like that.

The night at the 'Dillo when I'd killed with Joe, I'd ended up in the beer garden real late smoking a spliff with Steven. Joe had taken off and so had most of everyone else, but I wasn't ready to leave yet or to drive back west. I was riding the high of the night and I'd been there for hours and hours, it was late, and I looked up and it was just me and Steven, and I felt this sadness hit me and then stay in me and kind of throb in my chest. It was time to go after all. "All right, brother, nice to see you," I said.

"So good to see you, Doug. So good, man, you were so good," he said. His eyes were quivering shut and I felt the sadness again, pounding in my body like it was moving around through my veins.

"You got a car?" I asked.

"Oh yeah, of course," he said. He fished around for his keys in his pocket but came up empty. "Huh," he said. He looked at me. I stood up.

"I'll drive you," I offered, even though it was the last thing I wanted to do. I couldn't well leave him digging for his goddamn keys in the gravel or sleeping in the lot.

"Oh, that's very Doug," he said. "Very nice," he corrected himself. He held the spliff in his hand.

"Let's go now, though."

"Yessir," he said but didn't budge, didn't move an inch. I stood up and waited a minute, but he still wasn't coming.

"Come on, brother," I said, "I'm gonna drive you." I walked around the table and patted his back a couple times pretty hard. I was still high and buzzed too, but I was fine as long as I got out of there. The floodlights were on and everything was lit up too bright. I longed for the cab of the truck. "We gotta go."

He came to a little bit and followed me best he could out the gate of the garden and through the lot, but the big puddle I'd avoided on my way in was still sitting there and the kid walked right through it, barely even lifted his feet so that the water had a little wake behind him and his jeans were splattered with mud and clinging to his boots.

"Goddammit," I said, but he didn't seem to get that I was saying it to him, or about him, and once we got in the truck he brightened up some and managed to tell me roughly where he lived, not too far south, back behind Oltorf past the greenbelt where it dips. I nudged the truck out of the lot easy as I could and looked around for cops. I pulled onto Riverside and made a right at Congress and rode it south and saw the streetlamps on the bridge and the strip of downtown lit up like a dream in my rearview. Little city. Steven was asleep with his head against the window and his arms crossed around his body. I felt sorry for the kid, he was really out of it. Somehow I knew too that I was going to feel like apologizing for this next time I saw him, so that he wouldn't feel too guilty. I always felt that way when somebody else was as blasted as he was. I'd want to apologize, just for seeing it, even though I wasn't doing anything wrong at all. But now I just had to keep my eyes on the road, and I must've done twenty-five all the way up the hill and past Donna's Club and made a right on Cumberland. It was shit down there, and it felt even worse than usual that late on a Sunday night. Most of the houses were barely standing, and you could see the waterlines cutting clean across the outsides of some of them from when the creek had flooded during that storm Dee had been talking about, the tropical thing, and it had been almost a decade since. I tried to drive faster so I wouldn't have to see it all, the fences with holes eaten out of them and those steel bars over the windows and every once in a while a man walking too slow down the sidewalk. I eased down Stacy, which was all I could get out of Steven's mutters to me, and when I couldn't wake him up by yelling at him, I had to pull over to the side of the street and shake his shoulder. "Bud," I said, "which one is it?"

"Huh?" he asked.

"This your street here? Which house?"

"Oh," he said. "I can just get out, appreciate it."

"I'll take you to the house if you just tell me which one's yours."

"Down farther," he said. "Down there." He pointed out the windshield. I kept driving, until he signaled for me to stop by throwing his hand out in front of him. He looked around in the truck like he had something to take with him, but he had everything in his pockets. "What a night. *Great* night. See you real soon, man, tomorrow maybe," he said, and he made a little clicking sound with his teeth, but he didn't open the door or anything.

"OK," I said.

Still, he just sat there. Out the windshield I could see a busted-up walk and a dark trailer. There was a whole sink, faucet and pipes and everything, just lying on its side in the yard—I could see it in my headlights. And I knew somehow that if I sat there for even one more minute, I'd lose every gasp, every ounce of good I'd had that night to a crushing wall of bad. It was too sad. Just everything was too sad, all at once. My heart was stuttering, and I wished like hell the radio worked, but it didn't, and it was so quiet in the truck.

"See you soon," I said.

He swiveled his head toward me fast, and for a second I thought he was gonna be sick right there on the dash. But he put his hand down on my leg, the one closer to him, on my jeans. He patted my thigh a couple of times, soft, so soft it hurt, and then he just left it there, for too long. I didn't want to look, but I thought maybe he'd closed his eyes.

"Brother," I said. I didn't want to be mean, I really didn't. "See you soon."

"See you soon," he said again, and finally, finally, he moved his hand and got out of the truck and started up the path. He was almost to the door, trying to keep his balance. And all I could do was put my foot on the gas and gun it, and I bet I was halfway to the stop sign at the end of the block before Steven even got his hand on the doorknob.

It'd been two weeks since that night, since the 'Dillo and the ugliness with Wendell. But he still seemed off somehow, and I could tell Deanna was frustrated with him too by the way she asked him for things real loud and sometimes cold. Plus, it was the perfect, early part of summer, when the light had changed back to the way it was supposed to be, and whatever was gonna bloom had bloomed. I didn't want to be worrying about Wendell. Friday night I'd gotten started on beers a little too early, and it felt like before me and the boys went on would be a good time to tell Wendell what I thought about him and the way he had been with me, ignoring me or otherwise making me feel shitty. Or at least I was considering it, saying something. I snuck out of a conversation to take a couple hits of a little joint in a circle out in the lot, and it calmed me down some.

The bar wasn't slammed yet but it was moving, and the doors weren't propped open, so the room felt busier than it was, all closed up with people and their voices and their cigarettes gathering up into a big cloud of smoke near the ceiling. I had a cigarette at a table near the stage with Hopper and Benny and a couple of guys Hopper knew and wanted to bring up to play in the back half of the set. I'd seen them play with Joe and Hopper at Threadgill's a couple of times, and they had real good horns in beautiful cases too. They had checked the sound for a minute or two earlier in the afternoon when they were miking up the stands, and they sounded real smooth, very clean and hot, and I couldn't wait to get them going during this cover of "Can't You See What You're Doing to Me" I'd been working on. The music felt good and new; the crowds were real. I was starting to feel some hope, some forward energy, and I thought if I could harness it right, Joe might hear it and make good on the hints he kept dropping about producing a record. Maybe, just maybe, this gig wasn't as far as I could go.

I was in a good mood, everything felt possible, except I'd been looking around my guitar a minute earlier and was missing a cable. It had to be somewhere close, but I'd looked all over the stage and down by the legs of the tables closest to it, and I couldn't find it anywhere. I knew I was gonna have to ask Wendell if he knew where it went, so I let myself finish my cigarette and then I told Hopper I'd be a second, grabbed my beer by the neck, and went hunting for him.

I could hear the clink of glasses being set up against one another in the rack under the hum of the juke when I came up to the bar, so I knew he was in the kitchen, and though I'd never gone back there during open hours, I'd also never been told not to or that it wasn't cool, and I needed to find my cable, so I slipped past Dee, and though she looked at me confused, she kept filling orders. She was wearing the jeans

I liked the most, real washed-out, and I took a look at how perfect they were sitting at the top of her hips. Not having babies had kept her real small and tight, and she looked good, but I was still in it with Wendell, and I really didn't want him to turn around and see me in the doorway gawking at his wife, so I kept moving into the kitchen. His back was squared up and his elbows were bent over the sink, his hands moving around in the water.

"Wendell," I said. "Hey, I'm missing a cord."

"Huh?" he asked.

"I'm missing my cable, and we're supposed to go on in ten minutes."

"Oh. Well, sorry."

I waited for him to say something else, but he went quiet. "You seen it?" I asked. "I don't know where it is."

"I don't have it," he said, still washing glasses steadily, dropping one after another into the rack at his side from too high so they were clattering.

"I didn't ask if you had it, man, I asked if you knew where it was." He wasn't talking, and I was losing my nerve a little because of it. "This is your bar, right? Seems like you're the one I'd ask if I was missing a cable. It was onstage earlier."

"This *is* my bar, Doug, ain't it? It *is* my bar."

"Wow, OK, man."

"I'm running my bar, and I sure as hell don't know where your goddamn cable is. Sure as all hell, I do not know."

I hadn't heard Wendell say so many words at once in a long time, plus this whole time he was being such a little *bitch* to me. He hadn't even turned around. And I'd been getting angrier and angrier even while being afraid to do anything about it, so angry I didn't really know what to do with my hands or my face, but I was just clenching them as hard as they could clench. I stood there a minute longer, gathering up all the force and strength I could, and I took a deep breath way down into my stomach like I was getting ready to really blow the hell out of a microphone but even louder than that, even louder, and I yelled, "Fuck you, Wendell." The *fuck* came out as hard as I'd ever said anything and even though my voice had kind of plummeted through the rest of it, the *fuck* echoed all over the room, off the tile and around us, and died slow and ringing until it was just the cold silence of the two of us standing there, and finally he turned around and looked at me.

I felt the bar go quiet outside too, and I was still in the doorway, and as I looked at Wendell's face, I thought I could feel Dee come over closer and I thought I felt her just standing there a couple of feet away breathing, but I don't know even now if she was really there or listening at all. Some old cheesy heartbreak song played tinny from the juke, but people'd stopped their talking and were quiet. So we were quiet too, just waiting. For a second or two Wendell and I just stared at each other. In that stillness he looked like something uglier than I'd seen, something cold. I'd never seen Wendell touch anyone, I realized, not intentionally. Not even Deanna—I'd never seen them touch.

His body seemed to gather all the way up into his full height—he got even taller—and I really noticed how close his head was to the ceiling. He had his hands down at his side, one of them on the bar rag he had tucked into one of his belt loops. He pulled it out of his jeans real slow and dried both his hands with it. He scraped his boots on the ground kind of like a horse, like he was kicking something up behind him.

I shouldn't have said anything to him, I should have just found the cable myself, I regretted it with my whole body and heart, I really did. Behind me I didn't know if Dee had moved back to the bar but I could hear the clank of bottles being pulled out of the well and slammed back in, and Hopper's voice lifted out and said something about a record and LA and the voices picked back up to their usual din, and they'd forgotten about us in the kitchen, staring at each other and just gathering up our feelings and wits around us. I was relieved. I hated being caught out of control like that. We were alone, at least. And then into the middle of all that anger and regret for having lost it, sidling up awkward behind my back and then squeezing his body around the side of mine, was the kid, was Steven. Fuck no, I thought. How'd I gotten to this place, with this kid? Where he was comfortable enough to come back here, get in between me and somebody else?

"Hey, Doug," Steven said. "Thought I heard something back here."

"Thanks, man, we're good," I said.

"Sure about that?" he said, and looked at Wendell. He couldn't even act like a man, this kid. It was like watching Jules playing dress-up when he was younger, like watching him run around the old yard in his little hat and rope stumps like they were cattle. It's the *acting* like a man that gives you away. The trying is what people see.

"We're sure," Wendell said.

"I was talking to Doug there, man, excuse me," he said, and my mouth went dry. I felt trapped, and all I'd been doing was looking for my goddamn cable. I couldn't play without it.

"Get out of the damn kitchen," Wendell said. Behind him the sink was still running, and I was worried all of a sudden that it was going to overflow, and then that would be my fault too.

"Come on," I said to Steven, but he didn't budge. He shook his head kind of gently, and his hair brushed from side to side around his face. He tucked it behind his ears with both of his hands, and he looked so silly there, so ridiculous.

"I think you might apologize to Doug. You might say sorry. He's why anybody comes out here after all," the kid said, "to hear him play."

Wendell stood there.

"I mean, you might as well thank him. For all he's doing," Steven said.

"All he's doing," Wendell repeated, real quiet and slow.

"Yeah, man, I mean, he's doing a lot for you, don't you think?"

"Shut up, man," I said to Steven, as mean as I could muster. "You're not helping. Shut your mouth now."

"Who is this?" Wendell asked, but I knew he knew, and I didn't know how to answer anyway. I felt really nervous with Wendell for the first time. He had a black kind of look in his eyes. I'd never seen him lose control, and I wasn't sure what would happen if he did.

"Let up," I said to Wendell, kindly, like I was on his side.

Steven had finally shut his mouth. I didn't want to touch him, not at all, but I made myself grab his shoulder with my hand, whip him around, and steer him through the doorframe, but then I couldn't push him anymore. He'd locked still and turned around and was about to say something else to Wendell, and the sink was loud and so was the bar, but I couldn't keep him from saying what he was going to say. Before he said it, he'd looked back at Wendell and then said, like he was talking to me even though he wasn't and we all knew it, he said: "What a sad old asshole."

And a glass hit the wall beside me and shattered into a thousand pieces, and the sound scared the hell out of me even though part of me had known it was coming that whole time. I felt a prick on my head and then a little heat, and I reached into my hair and pulled out a little piece of glass, so small in my hand I wasn't sure how it'd even cut me. I looked at the floor, and the bottom of the glass was sitting there jagged but still together and right side up, like I could pick it up and drink out of it if I didn't mind cutting my lips all to hell.

Deanna appeared in the door, and I'd been waiting for her, I realized, but when I turned toward her, she had a look on like the one she got when people she knew walked their tabs: more surprised than angry or disappointed. Wendell took one more short look at all of us and turned his back and plunged his hands into the sink. There wasn't anything else to do. Steven followed me like a dog to the table, and when we got back over, Benny had my cable in his hand. It'd been coiled behind the kick drum the whole time.

You know, to be honest, most of what I remember about that weekend was the crowd. The people. Rush Creek *packed*. Like we'd rallied the troops, called up an army somehow. Man. They just kept coming. There were so many people I wasn't sure why I was thinking about Wendell anyway, and later that night, when everybody was good and wasted, he had come out quickly and pulled me aside to say he was sorry for throwing the glass, and he did really look sorry, ashamed. Deanna was trying not to look over from the kitchen doorway; she turned away all awkward and sad. I'd been working on forgiving him already. I knew he wasn't trying to hurt anybody anyway.

I felt keyed up still, though, so I stayed real late. Almost everybody stuck around, and we played a short third set even, after Wendell left, so the bar was rocking until almost one thirty, and then we mulled around until Deanna finally put her foot down and said she couldn't keep serving if anybody wanted the bar to be open the next day. Or later that day at this point, she guessed. The line at the bar to close tabs was insane, and I still didn't want to wander home and get that late-night kind of sad with Gwen asleep and somehow annoyed at me anyway, and Jules sprawled out sweating on his bedspread, didn't want to be that kind of lonesome. Or I wanted to stave it off as long as possible, anyway. I found a table in the corner a whole group of guys had just left, the table a mess of bottles with the labels scratched off in stripes and leaving wet little wakes on the vinyl. I picked one up, and it was half full and still relatively cool, so I started to take a swig and almost did before I noticed two butts floating on the surface when I sloshed it around. It reminded me I needed a smoke, but it took me searching every damn pocket I had to find a crushed Marlboro in the chest of my jacket with the filter barely hanging on. I lit it anyway. I had to hold the crack in the paper together with my fingers.

Benny was headed over, eyes popping out his head. He sat down across from me. "Shit," he said.

"What's going on?"

"Oh, nothing," he said. "Too little."

"Sure," I said. I peeked in a couple of the other bottles and took a warm sip of somebody's spit out of one.

"God," I said.

"Christ, you're really that lazy?" Benny asked.

I gestured at the line of people trying to close out. But Benny opened up his jean jacket and, like magic, there were two Heinekens tucked into the inside pockets.

He passed me one. "I'm your little angel tonight," he said.

"Devil, you mean," I said.

"What I said." He clinked the neck of his bottle against mine.

"Anybody left around?" I asked.

His eyes glittered, and I wondered if he wasn't liking Steven just a little bit more now that he'd started to bring coke with him every night. I had no clue where Steven was getting it at first; there was no way he had cash to spare. But I'd sorta mentioned to Hopper the week before that I wasn't sleeping great—the house didn't have AC, and it had started to get so hot in the bedroom I was sweating deep pools into the mattress every night—and he'd slipped me a pill, told me Steven had given him a baggie of them he'd gotten off his roommate, who had some kind of in. Everybody was grateful, sure, but goddamn if the kid needed another reason to parade around the way he did.

I'd taken a bump or two off the edge of Benny's pick between sets a couple of times, but I really had tried to ignore it as much as I could. The drinking was enough to get me through even a long night, and it was important to me to draw the line somewhere. But shit, had I ever seen Benny this warm and glowing? In years, even? Ever? It was so nice.

He was smiling big, fingering and tapping the lip of his beer. "Dee says she'll lock us in."

"Really?"

"She's in a kind of mood."

"What mood?" I asked.

"You know I don't give a shit what mood. It's just a mood, I can tell," he said. "But she'll lock us in if we want. I mean probably not literally, but you know."

"She's gonna stay and serve?"

"My sense is she's gonna stay and drink. You need to be *served*? I'll serve you."

"Wish somebody would," I said. I scanned the room so Benny wouldn't see how happy I'd gotten at the idea of Dee staying.

The tab line was moving now, and T.K. was sopping up old liquor from the rail with a series of rags and tossing them back behind him. I could hear them slap the floor and wondered if Hopper was somewhere around to hear it—I'd been on him about getting his bass stickier on "Moving," and I hadn't been able to show him what I meant. The door opened and creaked closed over and over. And suddenly the loneliness was creeping up on me anyway. I spotted the back of Steven's oily head, and it was only the hope that Dee really would stay and slum it with us that kept me in the bar, but it did.

"OK," I heard her say as loud as she could. "Y'all all staying?"

"Only if the girl is," Benny yelled back.

I could see Dee look around, clock the dozen people left, look to see who he was talking to.

"I'm talking about you, baby," Benny said, and I could see her face flush clear across the bright room.

"I'll stay a minute," she said, "so y'all don't fuck anything up too bad."

"I've never fucked up anything too bad in all my life, say you're sorry," Benny said back.

Hopper emerged from near the front and stood up and saluted Dee, all upright. He came across the room toward us.

"Look it, Ringo's on the move," some girl said.

Hopper stuck up a middle finger. He'd take her home, I was pretty sure.

Everybody kinda settled down around our table and a couple others nearby. Steven was up against the pool table, perched anxious on the edge. Hopper's girl and her friends looked at one another like they weren't sure where to sit, what to do with their hands. They seemed so young somehow. But I never know what to do with my hands, not unless they're on a guitar, and I felt warm toward them. I was trying to harness the warmth, trying to hold it real close and give it to everybody with my eyes. I thought it might make me feel better to treat people especially good. I thought it might help me turn the bad feeling around, I mean. I saw Dee walk toward us with a bottle of whiskey and a handful of shot glasses, drop them off, and then head to the back door to peek outside before she bolted it.

Then Benny was up out of his chair, headed to the stage.

"Benny, y'all can't play," she said, walking back over. She did look off to me then, a little sad and a little edgy.

"What you talking about, we can't play, lady? I, for one, think we play pretty damn good."

"No, I mean," she said, "it's too late."

"Too late for the *sound*?" Steven asked, all dreamy, and then he giggled.

"Shut the fuck up," Benny said.

"Be nice," Hopper said.

"*Please* shut the fuck up," Benny said. "Don't worry, Deanna, we'll play real soft."

But I didn't want to play anymore. I'd been playing all night and I was way past drunk now, and my head was done in, and I couldn't think of a single song I loved all of a sudden. Not one. How was it only Friday night? Benny was back next to me with my Martin and an unplugged Telecaster. Could I just be there? Could I just get it and calm down and not get washed away by the tide, the feeling of sadness just closing in on me? I wasn't sure. I looked at Deanna, and my vision blurred, and I saw my mother when she was young. And Gwen, when she was younger. And then, oddly, Steven. Steven's face, still young. Not in a bad way, exactly. Not really. A kaleidoscope.

"Any requests?" Benny asked. I took a shot of whiskey with my left arm over the frets. The acoustic was just deadweight on my legs.

"Never mind," he said, then looked at Steven even though Steven hadn't said a word. "I don't give a shit what you want to hear." He was playing the Telecaster like a bass, plucking the notes out one by one, as if he were ripping them out of the dirt that sprouted them. It sounded all right, real pokey and dry without a pickup. A little shuffle. Hopper was beating on the edge of the table with his hands.

Oh, I had it. The D dropped. I had it. This old Lightnin' Hopkins song I used to play when I was down, real down, back before Gwen and Jules and this crazy-ass bar, back before anything, "Life I Used to Live." I wasn't sure what it would do to me now, but I played the riff real high and tentative, as slow as I wanted, and Benny would know it— it had been on his list too, when we met, when we weren't much more than kids—and I sang the first line in the G, even though I knew it'd get too low for me before long. *Who cares what's coming?* I thought. *Ain't nothing but now.*

"*You know the life I used to live. Lord.*"

I said it over and over, through one measure, two measures, three damn times. "*Lord. Lord. L—*" Benny played gentler than I wanted him to, and I could barely hear Hopper's eighths.

"*I ain't gonna live it no more. You know the life I used to live. Lord.*"

The world stopped then, while we played. Everything stopped. Felt like nobody was breathing, even, all these people around me still and close, Benny and Hopper and the girls with their hips, and that guy T.K. had brought out a couple weekends in a row who thought he could bass as well as Tulsa, and I guess he could, but not by ear, and you know, Hopper's cousin nodding his big old bald head with a pool stick in his hand, and I felt a weight come down, a pressure from above me. All these people looking at me like I had something to give them, like holding out their hands for it, and the big, deep fear that I didn't have it to give. There wasn't a single person I wanted to play for. Not but for maybe Deanna, who didn't ask me for much at all.

And then, you know, right in the second bar of the solo, which I was keeping real easy because there was a part of me that thought I might cry right along with the hammers and bends, I saw her stand up and give me a little half wave and walk out the door. I had to sing the line about saying goodbye then too, like somebody had planned it out, and I felt all my bones sink down into the chair, which sunk down into the floor, which was set down into the ground, and I wasn't sure I'd ever be able to stand up again. Hopper still beating on the table, and a half-full glass wobbled and tipped over. My hands were numb, but they played anyway.

And afterward, after Benny had taken the girls out to the lot, and while Hopper was packing up the gear we didn't need to lock in the closet, that was when Steven came up to me. Sat down, leaned toward me. Cut two long lines on the table, pulled a dollar bill out of his front pocket and rolled it up real tight, handed it to me.

Yes, please, I thought, snorted one of them.

"Dougie, can I ask you something?" he said real quiet. I'd handed the bill back, and he was twirling it in his fingers.

"What?" I asked. I thought I saw Hopper take a glance over at us and then make himself busy again.

Steven's jean jacket was half on, one sleeve in, and the rest of it was hanging off his shoulder like a robe or an old Greek toga or somewhat. "I'm sorry," he said.

"Sorry for what?"

"Oh, nothing," he said.

"Well," I said.

"Do you believe in that stuff?" he asked quickly, looked sidelong at me.

"What stuff?"

"That song, you know. Church. God and stuff." He bent down and snorted the line left on the black. He gasped, a big inhale like he was pulling in all the world. "You believe in it?"

"No," I said. My head was a balloon, swollen and drifting. I felt the last couple of weeks—Steven against the stage with his face busted open, the guitar in my lap at the Armadillo, the crowds getting bigger and Wendell quiet—close in on me, lick at my heels. It felt like the world had built up into something new without me realizing it: like I was inside a weird, minor bridge in a song I'd assumed would stay square and easy. I was in the long second before the drums come back in, when all there is to do is wait and sense and be. The best songs—the real, old-school Texas blues or some of the new stomp around town too, sure, some of it—know exactly how long to make you sit there before launching back into key. But if you don't know what you're doing, it can go on too long. And then it's too much, way too much, to sit through. It starts to eat you alive, that waiting. You start to beg, pray, for some goddamn closure, for the chorus to come.

"Yeah," Steven said. "OK."

That cross still around his neck, swinging, swinging when he leaned down. Hopper was gone now.

Who were we again? Me and this kid? Who exactly? I wanted him to tell me, but I didn't know how to ask.

"You sure?" he asked.

"No," I said again. I looked at his hands.

TWO

I left here once. I did. It matters to me that I left, though these days it doesn't serve me much to talk about it. Now everybody wants to stay here instead.

I always thought it was easy to tell the people who'd never once left town. As a girl it made me embarrassed for them. You could hear it in how people talked, see it in how they moved, their forever roots, the unyielding sameness of it. There was something too delicate about everyone I knew in Austin, like they were expecting a cousin around every corner, like they were just sure they'd get whatever kind of help they needed. They seemed to me wide-eyed and too forgiving. That, or they were angry in a childish way, like my mother, mad at the world for not giving them the kind of respect they thought they deserved, seething at night under their covers. Sometimes they were both, simultaneously. I didn't want to be that way. All I wanted was somewhere else. I wanted to come *back* home—twice a year at first, out of some ancient obligation to my mother, and then eventually only at Christmas. Two days, or three. I'd complain to an old, stuck friend over stringy chicken-fried steak, complain about the roads and the way people moved so slow, drip-slow—and didn't they have somewhere to be, something to do?—until they wanted me gone again. I didn't even want to mean it necessarily, I wouldn't have. I just wanted to be able say it. I wanted to come back from some real city, Chicago, or Atlanta, wander just barely into the scrub till I could see the creek, dry and same as ever, and feel proud that I'd gotten myself to another place, a place where time passed loud enough you could hear it.

So I left. I was sixteen, still a kid. I left with Wendell, who'd come into my mother's candy store on a drive from Midland to Houston, bought a dozen pieces of divinity I'd rolled back and forth into logs over a field of pecans, bent his big body down, and asked too loud right next to my ear, smelling faintly of diesel and grease, if I wouldn't like to meet him for a Coke down the road in a couple of hours. If I could get away. It didn't seem to matter to him much one way or the other if I showed, which is mostly why I went. The shop stank of gin and sweat and sugar, and my mother wouldn't notice me leave anyway.

I closed my eyes, standing there on the front porch of the house I'd grown up in. It was only noon, and I'd been up at the bar an hour already, even though I hadn't left until at least three or three thirty the night before. Given T.K. the keys to lock up after the boys and drove home with heavy legs and a catch in my throat. Now the boards of the front porch pitched a little more than they used to under my feet; I thought for just a moment that I could feel the spin of the earth, and I opened my eyes again.

The house felt trapped in time. Sun flitting through the cedars and the little bunches of leaves on the live oaks. Light dappled and bleeding all over the place like watery paint. From the porch, if I squinted, I could almost see the shape of the storage shack we'd torn down to build the bar—the old star, even, the one without the neon, propped against the side, steel and the points so sharp they'd rip your sleeves open. The driveway winding its zigzag out to the road. I came over to the house as little as I possibly could. Walking across the lot too far made me feel queasy, haunted. I thought my mother might still be there, sitting in the living room on her chair and acting like she was reading a book, though I knew she was just staring at the words on the page and holding it splayed open on her lap so that she'd have something to hold that wasn't shaped like a highball glass. Quiet, yes. Endlessly.

Wobbly there on the slats, I'd become all the things I didn't want to be anyway. I'd come back home. Got soft and angry in the end—just had put it off for a while was all I'd done—walked right back into the mire I came out of, and deliberately. I could feel my blood running, and I felt grateful to Wendell suddenly, grateful that he'd lost his temper the way he had the night before, in earshot of a full bar, grateful he'd accidentally given me a way to break up the day, a reason to see Doug.

Doug had come into the living room at some point, and I could see him through the curtains in the front window. He was standing there shirtless, moving something off the back of a chair, and I saw where his hair fell on his shoulders, the ends of it. The divot of muscle above the butt of his jeans. He wasn't small exactly, but he was tight and somehow smoother than most men I knew, moved silky. My breath hitched, just a little, before I saw him feel me there, my eyes on him, and he started and turned and looked over his shoulder. I tried to fix my face to look like I'd just now climbed the steps, and I gave him a little wave. He scrambled and padded to the door and invited me in.

Doug seemed nervous too—more nervous than usual—but I couldn't really tell until I sat down on the couch and he came back in with coffee. When he tried to set a mug down in front of me it spilled all over the table. It was Doug and Gwen's table, if you could even call it a table; it was a pallet, really. The coffee leaked down through the holes of it and onto the little rug underneath.

"Don't worry," Doug said. "Don't you worry. I got it." He left to get a rag.

I looked up at the ceiling while I waited for him. I worked hard not to look around too much or focus on anything for too long. Wendell had really cleaned the place out years ago, when I finally put my mother in that home in Brentwood—and then again, real briefly, before Doug and Gwen and Jules came out to live in it. The big curtains had come down, and he'd put up new panels too light and gauzy to block out anything. And at some point he'd painted the molding this oddly bright white, blinding white, which gave the room a half-finished feeling and only drew attention to how long it had been since anything else had been painted. There was a hint of the old smell still, the same smell as always: booze and gravel dust and the heavy of my mother's rose perfume. Though now there were books everywhere, tossed in piles and stacked up against the wall. I heard Doug coming back.

"I'm so glad you came by, Dee," he said. He kind of tossed a rag on top of the spill and moved on, picked up a guitar off the chair by the neck and propped it against the wall, and it swayed a little. He sat down across from me. He scratched his chest, and too hard—I could see his fingernails burn paths into his skin. "You know, because I was thinking about you. Not in a bad way," he said. "I just mean I wish we had more talks together, more chats. I feel like you and I are on the same wavelength, kinda, you know what I'm talking about? I like hearing what you think about things. I've been thinking a lot about wavelengths, a lot." He smiled at me, genuinely, but then he glanced behind him at the doorway like he was waiting for somebody else. I shifted my weight forward to start to wipe the spill as subtly as possible.

I knew a good deal about Doug now. I knew what whiskey he liked, and the smoke and a half he needed to have alone before he could start a set, and he'd even spent an off night a couple weeks back sitting on a stool, talking about—or trying to talk about—how badly he wanted to get in a studio with Hopper and Benny, how he wanted another shot at making a record. It'd been surprising he'd said even that much. He'd start sentences he wouldn't finish, and I had to do a lot of piecing together on my own to figure out what he was really trying to tell me. I'd learned Doug would do a hell of a lot—anything, it seemed—to avoid talking about how he really felt, what he really wanted. I knew he had to dodge and hustle to keep so light and easy all the time, to keep being Doug without any breaks.

"Wavelengths," I said with a little tease in my voice. I didn't mean it to be there. I was so tender with him most of the time—it had just happened the moment I met him. I wasn't like that, really, not with anyone.

He looked ashamed.

"No, no," I said, "tell me about these wavelengths."

"Well, it's just about getting along. Or thinking the same way." He bobbed his head up and down. Doug was always rocking a little.

"Sure," I said. "Kindred spirits."

"*Exactly*," Doug yelped, like I'd said something brilliant. His hair was a little matted, I noticed then.

"Been, uh, reading?" I asked, and half gestured around.

He laughed a little too long. "No, no," he said, "those are Gwen's. She likes them more than people usually. Lucky she slums it with me."

"Did Wendell get you bad last night?" I asked quickly. I didn't much want to talk about Gwen.

"Nah," Doug said. He ran his hand over his scalp and then down through his hair. He started working out the knots at the bottom and then stopped just as suddenly. "He just got upset, you know," he said. "He didn't throw it at me anyway,

I could tell, he meant to hit the wall. Plus, we've all been there."

He smiled.

We were both quiet for a minute. I didn't much want to talk about Wendell either.

"I thought you might stay longer last night," he said.

"Oh, yeah, well. Just got late." I couldn't tell how he'd meant it—if he just said it to say something, or if he'd cared when I'd left. Could he have wanted me to stay? I waited, swallowed, tried to find his eyes. But he didn't say anything else. His foot kicked the leg of the chair once, and then again.

"How are you doing?" I took a chance. "I mean, really, you know, up here? With the bar and the gig and everything?"

"I'm great," he said. "Everything's great!" He popped a knuckle. "I'm just a little blitzed from last night still. Nothing to write home about. I just drank *a lot.*" He kind of stage-whispered the *a lot,* like I hadn't been there serving him. "You know, I think I lost some of the night, actually. That's damn embarrassing, ain't it?"

"You lost it?"

"Oh, the end of it's a little blurry, I mean."

He sounded off, and he wasn't looking at me. Whatever he was upset about, it wasn't the argument with Wendell, I was pretty sure.

"The best thing is that I woke up with a little riff in my head," he said. "You ever woken up with music in your head? Makes it all worth it. Really makes it all worth it."

He started to get up and move toward the guitar, but he

winced and sat back down. "Ooh boy, that medicine ain't doing much for me yet," he said. "Still, did I tell you how happy I am you came to say hi? Makes a man feel good."

"An old lady showing up on your porch? You're an easy sell."

"What? What are you talking about?" he asked. He responded to my jokes seriously like that, like I couldn't possibly be kidding about anything. I didn't know what to do with it. "You're not old."

"I'm not young," I said, and peered at him. His eyes were wide and blue, and he held my gaze longer than I expected him to. I could feel my heart beating like it was caged. I felt exposed, open. When he looked away, my stomach swung low.

I knew we were past the point in the conversation when we could've really talked to each other about anything big. About Wendell, about more than just the glass he'd thrown. About the smaller miseries, I mean, of a marriage I'd let wilt so long without water it was too brittle to touch, or about whatever Doug had or had not forgotten about the end of his night. I could feel the hope of a more intimate conversation floating through the room and then right out the front door when it opened. I heard soft feet in the foyer, and then I saw Gwen's head peek through the door. Before she adjusted, I got a real quick glimpse of her true reaction to finding me there in her living room with Doug in just his Wranglers. I'd never gotten along that well with other women. Men were so much easier to read. Most of them, at least. Women scared

me a little: I never knew what they wanted from me. But this
time it was clear as water, and I knew for certain that Gwen
didn't want to find me there. I saw it pool in her eyes, even
though she'd already dredged up and planted politeness on
the rest of her face.

"Hey, Dee," she said.

"Shit, hey, baby!" Doug said, stood up. "How goes?"

"Julian built a fort down there by the creek, he was showing me. You should go see it," she said. "It's impressive,
actually."

We'd named the bar after the creek. Silly. An old joke.
The creek runs bright blue on the maps, but the bed stays
dry almost all year. Even a big storm just sits there the next
day like an old puddle, still and ridiculous. You had to dig
through thick clots of cedars and prickly grasses to get down
to the bank, but it wasn't far at all really, and in the late summer you could walk right down the dry bed and not know
it was anything but a holler. But there might've been some
water now, just maybe, running through the scrub from the
north.

"Tell him to be careful," I said before thinking about it.

Gwen looked at me with her eyes fiery. I knew Jules had
been running around back there, and late too, while she was
paying no attention at all. I'd see him sometimes at night
between sets, out the back door, like an animal right at the
edge of the tree line. Midnight with all those cars in the lot.
I judged her for it, but what did I know about being a mom?
I'd never wanted to know.

"Oh, thanks, he's fine," she said. "Actually, Doug was supposed to come down about an hour ago. Julian's down there waiting to show him."

"Shit," Doug said. "I forgot. I'm sorry."

I stood up as if to go, but I stopped a minute and watched them. He was standing in front of her with his back to me. "Shit, I'm sorry, baby. I just forgot. Wanna go back out with me now?" His head dipped down and he kissed the top of her head, and she seemed truly surprised. "I'm sorry," he said again, and hugged her to him.

Over his shoulder I saw her face, taken aback but happy too by his big warmth. It occurred to me looking at them that he might have been apologizing for something else, something bigger than forgetting about Julian. It was so hard to look away. I watched her little hands slide over his back, cup his shoulders, her palms pressing and wandering, her fingers playing on his bare skin. I bustled around, like I had something to grab, which I didn't, not even a pack of cigarettes, and made to leave.

"You don't have to rush out," Gwen said to me with some effort.

"Oh, no," I said. "I really just came by to—" But I couldn't think of anything. Why *had* I come by? They both looked at me, waited.

"Just wanted to check and see if y'all needed anything, really," I said. "With the house or—"

"That's sweet," Gwen said. "I think we're doing fine. We're really grateful to both of you." She sounded sincere.

"Good," I said. "Just let me know, you know? Or Wendell too, he'd be happy to help with anything."

When I made my way around them, awkwardly, and toward the front door, Gwen was still touching him, but Doug was cracking his knuckles again, one by one, and looking past her, like he'd forgotten she was there. All marriages are difficult, I guess, after all. I'd only ever had the one.

I had to run another load of cup towels. I had to stack and dolly the Pearls to get them in from the back storage. I had all this shit to do before we opened, but when I walked back across the lot from the house, fast, like somebody was watching me, all I could think about were Gwen's hands on Doug's back. I couldn't picture anything else. I was pretty sure that if I stopped, stood still, I'd feel the play of her fingers on my own skin—sizzling, light. The air felt charged too, outside sure, but even when I pulled open the door and stepped back into the dark of the bar, that electric feeling followed me.

I wanted it to. It was in the sour smell of the vinegar I used to wipe down the booths in the back—it stung my nose—and it was in the burn of the ice on my hands where I had picked at my nails. I tried to feel the feeling just enough, enough to feel its heat but not so much that it'd disappear. I opened both doors, and the light shone in through the skinny little wisps of dust, and I had it all to myself, all of it, just for a second, and then I heard Wendell's boots ticking through the gravel in the front. A little faster than usual too, but there was no mistaking them for anything else: he'd always planted his heels too hard. It made me crazy to hear it, and the electricity around me dissipated and then cut off.

In the beginning, if I tried hard enough, I could remember finding Wendell's clumsiness charming. I'd been looking for loud when I met him. I believed he thought differently than regular people did. He was meant to be a hand on his daddy's ranch, but his grandma had told me later, half a bottle of brandy in and with him cooking her dinner even, that kid-Wendell couldn't keep a rope in his hands, or stay on a pony, or even tend a goddamn fire without threatening the whole acreage. But I knew they'd treated him special anyway, passed him around from chaperone to chaperone, just waited for him to get bored and want to leave on his own. He'd been the only son. When he first told me about working on the land, he talked about miles and miles of pasture—spread out wide and long like the gulf shore, he said. I was young enough I hadn't even seen the ocean, but I understood already that anybody who talked about hard work in metaphors like that was almost certainly absolute shit at doing it.

But the truth was he didn't think any differently than regular people did, I'd come to realize, and after longer than I should've, maybe. He just paid less attention. He didn't look around before he moved, and if he knocked over a whole table of beers when he threw them down, he'd let people sit there covered in it and kinda amble to the bar to get new ones, forget what he was doing along the way, and never come back. Wendell needed somebody to guide him through his life, a little perpetual hand on his elbow to get him across the room safe, clean up around him so he could keep moving, shepherd other folks gently out of his way. And in a way that could've been fine, actually. Some people are just like that, I guess: they need a bigger kind of help.

It could've been fine, except for how Wendell seemed to *expect* it. How easily he'd assume I'd fix whatever needed fixing—some lady sitting there with a puddle of Lone Star in the lap of her skirt—and at the same time insist, offended, that he would've gotten to it on his own, that he didn't need any help at all. How sulky he'd get if I even so much as reminded him to pick up a barstool he'd kicked over. I'd gotten used to the way people looked at him, how they'd play along nice enough for a while but wince at his voice and avoid his body as much as they could. I'd smile my apologetic, understanding smile. I could do that much. But I couldn't shake the feeling that Wendell was judging me somehow, and just for wanting to live without leaving a wasteland in my wake all the time, for wanting to move through the world with more grace than he did.

I'd left him at home, snoring like an old man on the couch, his feet hanging so far off it his soles skimmed the ground. When he came through the doorway into the bar, I was sitting at a table hanging chips on the clip racks. I lost him in the pit of sunlight and by the time I found him again he was already almost back behind the bar, squatting under the bridge instead of walking all the way around. I could hear his groan across the room.

"Hey," I said.

"I slept till one," he said.

"Yeah."

"OK," he said, exhaled. "I'm just sayin', you coulda woken me."

I'd had a mind to stay and drink the night before, I did, but I'd gotten sad. Really sad, all at once. Doug's voice without a microphone and the same slow chords in the hollow of 3:00 a.m.—I couldn't handle it. I needed the music he played to blow me out of my shoes, drums and amps and the crash of it, or I'd listen too closely and start to think about old sadnesses: trying to guide my mother into her bedroom before she passed out cold from the gin, every night untucking the sheet at the foot of the bed and taking her house shoes off so she didn't sleep in them. Her dirty socks. Every night thinking it might be her last, and she'd always said she didn't want to die with shoes on. Doug's voice and the plucky guitar, spare—and underneath it just that yawning loneliness, the soft and supple kind you might never crawl back out of. Wouldn't it be better with shoes on, anyway? Isn't it better to die living? T.K. was still around and could lock up, and I'd counted the cash. I wanted to stay, but I couldn't bear feeling that way. I drove home to Wendell.

He was asleep, but I could tell from his breath he wasn't fully out; some part of his mind was lingering, waiting for me. I stripped off my jeans, unhooked my bra, and rubbed my back gently where the strap had rubbed a rash into my skin. I needed to do something to supplant the grief—it'd clung to me like sweat the whole drive to our house, down through

Zilker and up the steep hill on Kinney. I waited for Wendell to stir, but he didn't quite. He was on his stomach, and I could see the muscles of his back rise and fall, even in the dark. I should've been more upset at him than I was for losing it with Doug, but it was a good reminder too that—despite all of him, the forgetfulness and the way he moved, and how long we'd been together—Wendell was capable of caring too much about something. Or losing himself over something, at least. I climbed on top of him and not soft at all, reached under his briefs and woke him up. If he was surprised, he didn't seem it. He flipped me over, and when he tried to take too long, play around, I dug my nails into him until he pushed hard enough to hurt me. It was too fast, though—he'd been right to try to slow me down—and he came before I could get in any kind of groove. Afterward I didn't feel the normal rush of tenderness for him, or the quiver in my feet, didn't feel anything but completely and totally exhausted. I'd made him finish the night on the couch, which was why he was back there angry and sighing, making a big show out of restocking the smokes. I stood up and went to hang the racks of Fritos, and then I went over to where he was kneeling in front of the cigarette machine. I put my hand as naturally as I could on the back of his neck.

"Hi there," I said.

He grunted and tensed underneath my palm.

"You wanna drink a beer with me?" I asked. I did feel bad for leaving him in the living room without saying anything. "Might be nice before the night starts."

He stood up slowly, stayed facing the machine. My hand slid down to his belt loop. He really was such a big man, so tall and broad; it could still surprise me.

"Body's stiff," he said.

"Let's have a beer. I got up here early, so everything's about done anyway." I moved back a step so he could turn around, waited. "Wendell," I said. "Look at me."

Still, he waited. He seemed like he was gathering energy for something, pulling himself together, and suddenly I felt really afraid something had changed, or gone for good. It occurred to me that he could leave me someday, if he wanted to. That he could just decide one day that he really would be happier without me. That he might think, like I did, about what it'd be like to touch somebody else. A surge of adrenaline shot through my arms, and my fingertips tingled.

"Baby, come on," I said, voice as steady as I could keep it. I felt desperate now. I had just said it to be kind really, but now I needed him to do it: to sit with me, to be with me. I didn't want to be alone. I needed him to turn around. "Have a beer and just let's sit for a minute."

Still nothing.

"Hey," I said. And I could hear the quake in it. "Please."

All at once he moved. He turned around fast, kissed my head without looking me in the eyes, and skirted around me. I held my breath, watched him go behind the bar and grab a bottle, crack the cap off against the ledge, and bring it back over. He handed it to me with two fingers and finally, finally, he looked at me. But his face was closed.

"I gotta clean up outside a little," he said. "Before it gets wild. Be back."

A clunk in my chest, and he was gone. I could feel the pressure in my head and I didn't want to start crying, so I drank that beer so fast the bubbles burned my throat, and it kept on burning, burning, until I cracked open another one.

Hopper was out smoking a cigarette under the pecan closest to the door. He smoked like he'd just come back from war, or from the 1920s, the cherry tucked delicately into his palm like a gift. In his big sunglasses, Hopper was especially beautiful. Glamorous, almost. You could have put Hopper straight onto a museum wall in Europe somewhere. His hair cropped close but wavy, disobeying however it could, and he had this wide smile that ran all the way across his face, and his bottom lip kind of fell out of it. When he was up onstage with Doug and Benny and whoever was playing bass or keys, or especially when he was mostly eclipsed by a pedal steel player in front of him, or that weekend they tried the sax up there, Hopper just peeking through on the beat, he looked stronger, surer, than the rest of them. He could be quiet when he wanted, but a couple of times I'd heard him get going, and that man could talk for hours—low and slow, like how you roast meat so it falls off the bone—about anything you wanted to talk about.

I'd just come out to plug in the star. It was only five or so and the sun wouldn't set till eight thirty, but people had started to drift in in groups already, and I wasn't sure when I'd get back out there to do it.

"Whatcha up to?" Hopper asked, and when I told him, he lodged his smoke in his lip and nodded.

"Gonna be crazy tonight, you think?" I asked. "I have a feeling." It was a stupid thing to say; it was Saturday, after all, and these past couple weeks it'd started to become clear Doug was turning into a real draw. And Joe was coming up more often; people followed him. I'd had three or four beers and a shot of well tequila that I'd had to force myself to gulp through the burn.

"Yes, ma'am," he said, and then clamped a hand over his mouth, cartoonish, gave me a sorry look, and smiled. "Fuck, sorry, I know you hate that shit. It just came out." But I didn't mind as much with Hopper when he pulled out all that gentility. I believed him; it didn't feel put on. I squeezed his arm lightly through his sleeve to tell him. I asked if I could bum a cigarette, and he pulled the pack out of his shirt pocket and gave me a kind of sly look to half ask before he lit it for me and passed it over.

"You seen Doug yet today?" I asked. I wanted to ask Hopper about the rest of the night, if something had happened after I'd left, or if Doug had just gotten careless the way he did sometimes, gone too late and too hard and suffered for it. But I wanted to ask offhandedly, like I'd just thought of it, so it didn't feel like I was poking. Just saying his name sometimes made me feel embarrassed. I took a deep drag off the smoke and felt my fingers shake a little.

"You know, I haven't," Hopper said. "But it's still kinda

early, huh? I thought maybe I'd just come up and have a drink and sit for a bit; it's so nice out."

It had turned into one of those days that are just so perfect they floor you. The radio on the drive up that morning had said it was supposed to rain, really storm at some point maybe, but there wasn't a single cloud in the sky. Ninety-two, ninety-three, but with a breeze. That impossible feeling, the wide-open, and the red clumps of late-season paintbrushes under the shade of the trees. It was the kind of day that slows people down, holds them in both hands, lets them forgive each other for whatever needed forgiving. Everything tastes better on those days, clean. You can be grateful for whatever you've got, grateful for Texas even, and not feel naive or blinkered or ashamed about it.

"Sure," I said. "How late did y'all stay last night anyway?"

"Too late," he said. "I need a break, to tell you the truth, but Joe's coming up tonight and he told Doug last week that maybe he's got time to produce a record. Doug doesn't want to bank on it, but Benny's like a dog with a bone. It'd be big for us though, you know. If it happens."

"Mmm," I said through the smoke. I didn't know why Doug hadn't told me himself. I felt a bolt of jealousy, and then felt angry at myself for feeling it. Wendell calls that my second feeling, the feeling I have about the first feeling. "Then I hope it happens," I said to Hopper, and smiled.

Before Hopper could even look over at me, a little Datsun truck pulled fast into the lot. I had to keep myself from ducking instinctively, it tore up so much gravel. It pulled into the new row somebody'd started, but three yards away from the next car over and too far in too.

"Damn," Hopper said. "He really can't drive that thing, can he?" He picked at something in his teeth. "It's a small truck, but still."

"Who?" I asked. The glare off the windshield was blinding.

"That kid Steven."

"Ah," I said. I could hear the disappointment in my own voice. "He's up here early too, huh?"

"Sure is," Hopper said, and his voice stayed even, but I could tell from how he said it that he didn't want to have to talk to Steven either.

We both just stood there for a second.

"The way some people hate him, it's something else," he said. "I mean, I get it. I do. But he does love the music, I mean, God, he really loves it. Which is nice."

Steven hopped out of the truck, slammed the door, and then immediately opened it again to grab something he'd forgotten, I guess.

"I don't hate him," Hopper said, firmly and quietly, like he was trying to convince himself of it. "And I don't wanna treat him bad, you know, but ain't like he helps himself either." And then, like he'd just remembered I was standing there: "Hey, how's Wendell doing? I heard he got a little wound up or something last night."

Steven was bounding toward us in overalls, just a little boy suddenly under the big old sun, and of all the people I wanted to have barging into any conversation about Wendell, or me, or anything really, Steven was near the bottom of the list. "No, he's great," I said too cheerfully. "He's inside."

I gave Steven as much of a hello as I could muster and turned to walk away, because under different circumstances I might have been able to talk to Hopper. About how stale things felt between me and Wendell—how the blue of it, the big drought of feeling, was both decades old and new every day. How Wendell embarrassed me and frustrated me and sometimes made me feel nothing at all, and how it all blurred together. How I needed him, and how I didn't. How I had no idea how to figure out how I really felt about him, after so long, and how I wasn't sure it even mattered if I did. I knew Hopper would listen, take me seriously. He was just like that. I could've asked him outright about Doug too, even told him how nervous Doug had acted when I'd seen him in the house. And Hopper wouldn't have misunderstood, and he wouldn't have gone off and talked about how I'd asked. He'd have respected me more than that.

"Hey, brother," I heard Steven say behind me, grating as ever, and Hopper gave him a little sound in return.

"I got lots for later," Steven said, and I could tell he was digging through his pockets. I dipped back into the darkness of the bar.

By six, we were absolutely slammed. Even with T.K. back there, and a couple extra kids we'd hired to barback, it was gonna be a goddamn marathon. Girls with their long braids and smoke so deep in their clothes you could practically touch it, swaying to the old records on the box. Wendell had refelted the table, and some guys in pearl snaps, everything clean and crisp like they'd walked off the set of a movie, were roaming around it like cattle at water. I saw one look over toward the corner where the box was between songs and soften when Patsy Cline came on. Wendell had disappeared somewhere—to clear some branches out of the lot, or to check inventory, or to hose off a stack or two of sticky folding chairs, I guessed, but I was about to really need him.

Seemed like everybody already knew it'd be a night. It depended on who we were up against in town, at the Armadillo or the Opera House, but on a Saturday like this, as perfect as it was, more folks would be willing to come out of town a ways. And if Joe showed up again, it was anybody's guess how it'd go. People were either better behaved, or they were much, much worse, when somebody more famous than Doug was around. The room would change, rev up fast, and sputter like an engine.

It was hard work to keep an eye open when we were that busy too. The redneck boys almost always started what got started, but Wendell was still fond of them. I was too, really, I'd known them forever. They lived west of the city, worked construction or for the county, needed a place to just unload and breathe. They wore their holsters, even if they left their guns in their trucks. They'd belonged here for a long time. You wouldn't have caught them in a crowd downtown. And they couldn't have named a blues song, or at least they couldn't have until a month ago. To them, I think, the music was a funny little anomaly—you could catch them peering like window shoppers at the stage sometimes when Doug was really soloing. The music wasn't the problem for them, I mean, and neither was Doug. It was the people the music brought out from town they couldn't stand. Sometimes it was hard to blame them. It feels awful to be looked down on so coldly by kids from somewhere else. Nobody owns any place, I know that, not ever, but it's impossible not to want something to feel like it belongs to you.

You could see it happening. I'd asked Wendell if he thought we ought to put T.K. out there even when we weren't taking a cover, just to keep things straight, so we got him to agree to sit out there instead of bartending for two bucks and a beer an hour. He came inside to watch the music too often, but he was six foot four and had been on that Reagan team that had won state, so he was better than nothing. He was always scowling too, and he wore that heavy ring on his right hand like a sleepy weapon.

Everybody drank. The girls in their skirts and the country boys who'd been around for years—they all drank. We were raking it in again. So, you know, we dealt with what came up when it came up. There was tequila to pour.

I looked around the room from behind the bar, and it was almost like I could see a new place taking shape around them. It was like a glow, sort of, or like how a certain kind of smell—oranges or smoke—would stick to your skin long after you'd peeled it or had a cigarette in your hand. It was in the way folks looked slowly around the bar: not to judge, exactly, but to be noticed judging. It was in the way they danced. Their nice boots and their denim. Someday I'd be the only one in the whole bar—tired and somehow, suddenly, old; old enough to have mothered some of these kids—who'd grown up in this town.

Where in the living hell was my husband? The rush was here. The sun would start setting in an hour or so—the doorway would turn that kind of deep pink, burst open—but I was so hot already I was losing my grip on the bottles. And taking stock then, I noticed Doug had snuck in without me seeing. And next to him, Gwen. And hell, Gwen barely ever came over. I met her eyes, and she blinked a little, and I knew that she had been watching me tend bar long before I noticed her. I looked around for a rag to wipe my hands, and I motioned at T.K. to tell him I'd be back in a second. I poured another shot, a little below the rim so I could carry it—I wanted to have it in my hand, didn't even know why—and made my way over to the booth closest to the door.

The way Gwen was sitting there on the vinyl I could see she didn't want to be where she was. When I got up close, I mean. Doug was squishing her all the way into the wall, and he kept touching her over and over again—her leg, her hair. I saw him reach up and tug once on her earlobe. It was even stranger for how close he was sitting to her, how she'd get pinned in a little more every time he moved. I wondered if he'd been like this all day long. Benny was sitting across from them with some waify blond girl whose eyes wandered and didn't meet mine once. I was hovering awkwardly over an empty chair at the end of the table.

"Hey, hey, hi," Benny said. "Doing good?" He was high already. His eyes were very, very wide: big gray marbles about to spin, looked like, right out of his face.

"Pretty good," I said, and smiled in his direction.

"Not bad in here," he said. "The people, I mean, pretty good crowd already." Then: "Good crowd!" again, loud and like he hadn't already said it.

"I just came over to say hi," I said, and looked at Gwen.

"Nice to see you on this side. You sticking around?" This side of what? I felt embarrassed for having left T.K. alone behind the bar and come over here. I felt embarrassed for saying it was nice to see her when I'd already seen her that morning. I felt embarrassed too because she knew it was a lie. And people were back there milling around, building up, waiting on T.K. to pour their liquor. I looked over and saw him wipe his brow dramatically, so I knew he was annoyed. Still, I kept standing there at the table.

"Gwen's gonna stay for the show," Doug answered for her. "How great is that? I told her I'd do something real special if she stuck around through the first set, didn't I, Benjamin?" He sounded genuinely enthusiastic.

"Call me that again, baby boy, and I'll knock your skull in," Benny said.

Doug smiled, leaned his head on Gwen's shoulder awkwardly.

I wondered why she was really here, and suddenly I wanted so badly for it to have something to do with me that I felt my back clench, and I stood up straighter. I looked at them, and the electric feeling was back, flickering and sparking, and I thought about them together—really together—when nobody was there to watch them. Touching each other. Their blood pumping at the same pace, their bodies pulsing and moving together, in the same bedroom my mother had slept in, under the same goddamn water spot on the ceiling I used to look up at while I stayed to make sure she kept breathing. I peeled my hair off the back of my neck, and my fingers felt like they belonged to somebody else.

"You're not leaving her much room," I heard somebody say, real clear and mean, and I realized it had to be the girl sitting next to Benny. Doug looked at her with the guilty eyes of a dog caught making a mess, but he didn't move. And then I saw Gwen reach up and wind her fingers through Doug's hair until her palm was kind of cradling his head lovingly, possessively, and he smiled huge.

"Well, that's great," I said to Gwen. "That you're gonna stick around."

Steven drifted up to the table from behind me, unsteadily, grabbing at the edge like he was on a raft just trying to reach the mainland. "Where's Wendell at?" Steven asked. Then he sat down heavy in the open chair. "Is he around?"

"You're looking for Wendell?" Doug asked. Gwen's hand was still in his hair, but his hands were in his lap. He seemed chastened somehow. I could see a new feeling flood his face.

Steven laughed, sort of. "Thought I might say hi, smooth things over."

"Hate to be the bearer of bad news," Benny said, "but Wendell's not your biggest fan. Friend."

"Wendell's over looking at the truck," Gwen said.

"What?" I asked before I could stop myself. I couldn't tell if that had been a jab or not. She kept her face blank.

"The clutch. He told me to head on over here about half an hour ago and leave him to it, guess it's not as easy of a fix as he thought."

I looked down at the little whirl of hair on the top of Benny's head, then looked down at the table, looked anywhere I could so I didn't have to look at Gwen. I hated her. For a moment, I let myself really hate her. I let myself hate Wendell too: the casual way he disappeared on me every time it mattered. It washed through and over me, and I felt cleansed, pure somehow. I felt wilder than I'd felt in a long time.

"Real good crowd, right?" Steven said. He scooted a little closer to Doug. I could see he wasn't right either, Steven. Even for him, he didn't seem quite right.

"You got some—" Benny said to Steven, and kind of wiped his own nose.

"Shit," Steven said, and ducked his head, used his T-shirt to wipe his whole damn face.

I didn't care about Steven or what trash was on his face. I took a deep breath, and then I looked straight at Gwen.

"I'm glad Wendell can help. With the truck," I said as kindly as I could, and even though I had no idea why he'd picked the beginning of a Saturday shift to try. Or why he'd gone over there without telling me, or if he'd ever gone over there before without telling me, or if he'd had other little conversations with Gwen while I was worrying about the back door sticking and trying to stretch out my hand so I could palm three beers instead of two. And suddenly I was imagining that she knew things about me, things about Wendell, and then that she'd told them to Doug, that they'd talked about us—pitied us, I mean—with their voices all soft, naked and young as teenagers under their sheets.

"Yeah, I think he will," Gwen said.

She lifted her butt off the booth and swung her hip into Doug to get him to stand up and let her out. "Ladies'," she said, and smiled at me gently.

Doug scooted out of the booth and made to stand. I saw Steven's head lolling a bit, and then I saw his hand reach over under the table and graze Doug's thigh. Put his whole palm on Doug's jeans and then slid it down his leg and off. It was tender, gentle and slow enough to notice. And I thought Doug would look down and do something, laugh at least. Something. It was a long enough touch it couldn't have been normal, and Doug had to have felt it. But you know, he didn't. Doug didn't do anything.

Occasionally I wondered why everybody had seemed to start to tolerate Steven, let him sit around with them all afternoon and late too, after the sets. The drugs he always seemed to bring now, sure. He'd started to strut. Still, I felt a wave of pity for Steven rise and crest in my chest. None of it felt funny like it sometimes could.

And then, while Gwen walked around Doug on her way to the bathroom in the back, and Steven readjusted his chair to get out of her way, and Benny and his girl were in each other's necks, and Wendell was apparently still across the lot with his body slid up under the engine of Gwen's Ford, and the tequila was still half-lodged in my upper chest, Doug met my eyes. There was no mistaking it for anything. Doug was scared, is what he was. He was afraid of something, and his look made me think I might be the one he wanted to talk to about it. Like he might need me in particular.

I made it through about six orders seething at Wendell and curious about Doug before I fished another longneck out of the trough, whatever was closest, and snapped the cap.

It was early enough people were still parking stupid, and I had to zigzag through the cars to get near the house. The hood of Doug's truck was up, and Wendell's boots were sticking out from under the chassis, just where Gwen'd said he'd be. I came around the front and nudged the sole of one of his feet, and he bolted up and smacked his head on the metal.

"Fucking Christ," he said, and wriggled his way out on his ass. He looked ridiculous, like a giant lizard in dirty Lees squirming out of a hole too small for him. He rolled a flashlight out with him, but the beam disappeared the moment it hit sun. "You scared the hell out of me," he said.

"What are you doing?" I asked.

"Draining the line."

"No, I mean, what are you *doing*?"

"I'm draining the line," he said again, and sighed.

"It's busy as all hell in there. Ignore me, I don't care, but come on, Wendell."

"You don't care?"

"*You* care?"

"I'm draining the fucking line so the clutch doesn't keep dropping to the floor, Deanna. I had a few minutes, and I told Gwen I'd help."

"Why didn't Doug ask you?"

"'Cause Gwen asked me."

"Great," I said. "So right now, Saturday night when we're slammed, is the perfect time to fix a truck that doesn't even belong to you. Absolutely."

He looked up at me from the ground, disappointed and condescending and not angry at all. "I'm tired. I slept like shit last night. What can I do for you?" he asked, and to be honest, I had absolutely no clue what I wanted him to do. I wanted him to need me. I wanted him to care enough to try to hurt me. I wanted to crawl under one of these trucks and look up at rust and hide there all night. I swallowed. We couldn't even talk to each other. The beer I'd grabbed was sweating down my hand and onto my wrist.

"I need you in the fucking bar," I said.

Wendell climbed to his knees, dusted off his thighs, and stood all the way up. He looped a greasy rag through his front loop, and his nails glistened with little rainbows of oil. We'd been like this for too long. I tried to tap some warmth from the pit of muck and contempt inside me, and I could, I could do it, but I had to hunt harder than ever for a vein.

"Well, then, let's go to the fucking bar," Wendell said, his voice barely a growl.

He glared at me, but after a minute his eyes drifted over my left shoulder. "What are they doing?" he asked.

"Who?"

He jutted his chin. I turned to look and saw Steven and Doug, standing under one of the oaks, facing each other, and Doug seemed to be looking down. Steven was, as ever, looking straight shamelessly at Doug. I was pretty sure Doug was just rolling a smoke, and they were standing out in the open, but the way Steven looked at him, it felt again like watching something I wasn't supposed to be watching. It was a subtle thing, and I was surprised Wendell'd noticed anything at all.

"I don't know. Smoking?"

"No," Wendell said. "By the door."

There was a big group of guys hanging out by the wall; one was sitting on T.K.'s stool, tipping it back and forth. Scooping gravel into their hands, three or four of them, picking out the biggest rocks and chucking them at Steven's back. They were mostly missing, I assumed, because the kid wasn't moving or turning around, but they were starting to really wind up, all of them in a line, like pitchers in a bullpen.

Wendell started off, heavy-legged, and I followed him. The closer we got to the bar, the clearer it was they were really pelting him. I saw one of Steven's hands reach up quick to rub the back of his neck. He wasn't going to turn around, I could tell, not for nothing. Somebody had taught this boy that ignoring trouble would get him through it, and I wondered who and when. Turning the other cheek doesn't do shit for a man whose whole face is already busted.

Doug had a smoke hanging off his lip, unlit, and he seemed frozen in place, and I saw Steven move toward him, like he was going to light the smoke for Doug, and only then did Doug flinch, jerk like he was moving away from a snake.

I heard a voice from the doorway, Hopper's, saying, "Are y'all fucking children or what? You need Daddy to tell you to stop it?"

Benny behind him, coming out with a glass in his hand, and Steven's back still to everybody, slouching now.

"What is it about you that makes people want to throw shit at you?" Benny yelled at him.

"I think I know," Benny's girl singsonged.

The guy sitting on the stool waved at Wendell when we walked up, and Wendell stopped for just a second, gave the guy a stare. "It's gonna be a goddamn long night, ain't it?" he said to me over his shoulder—or to himself, I couldn't tell— and I watched his broad back disappear inside.

The guys had stopped with the rocks, but even with Hopper and Benny out there lighting a joint, they were still looking around for trouble. I saw one of them, young but going bald already, his hairline like a low wave way out on the water, light a smoke and tuck the soft pack into his shirt pocket, and then he reached over and knocked the hat backward off one of his friends, and the friend said, "Fuck you," took a swing at him, a right hook he pulled at the last second, and everything dissipated a little. I saw a low bank of dark red, a clot of blood near the horizon, and thought we might get that storm anyhow. I was ready for it.

"Hey, hey," Doug said, and he motioned at me to come over.

"Mm-hmm," Steven mumbled in my direction.

"Joe's coming up here tonight," Doug said. "Gonna pull him up to play a little, just so you know, probably both sets. Might be louder than regular, but he's doing us a big favor maybe, so if you don't mind." He said it so softly I knew he cared more than he wanted anybody to think he did. He cared so much he didn't want to talk about it at all. He looped his arm around my shoulder and pulled me in to his side, and I could feel the frizz of his hair against my cheek.

"I heard," I said, soft. "Congrats." This was the closest I'd ever been to him, and he smelled like musk and man, and I couldn't breathe right. I leaned into him as much as I could without losing my balance, and I could feel his rib cage through his shirt.

"No, he deserves it," Steven said.

"Sure," I said.

"He deserves it more than anybody," Steven said again, and took an uneven step toward both of us, caught himself, and I felt Doug's forearm tense up on my neck.

"OK, well, I gotta get back there, then," I said, but I stayed where I was, tucked into the pocket of him. I wanted to stay there forever.

"I'll go in with you," Doug said. He pulled away from me like it was nothing and tossed his smoke.

"Good to chat, brother," he said to Steven, and it was oddly cold the way he said it, after they'd been standing there together like that, and Steven's sadness yawned open from his eyes and took over his face. He scratched the back of his head long and hard and smiled through it.

"Onward and upward," Steven said, and he trailed behind a couple feet, but he wasn't gonna stay out there alone for nothing.

I couldn't bring myself to look at Wendell, so we just sort of worked around each other, gave room. The bar was four-deep for another half an hour. A guy in a tank top, gray hair, and a long silver necklace that dragged on the bar when he leaned over had asked for five shots of Johnnie Walker Black, which was the dumbest thing I thought I'd ever heard, shooting Scotch like that. But hell, I'd pour them if he was paying for them. I caught Wendell in my peripheral vision while I was lining up the glasses, and I was overcome with a sorrow I couldn't even hold. I had to steady myself against the rail, and I poured good whiskey all over the wood. The guy snickered at me and then jolted forward—somebody behind him had knocked him in the back for taking so long and not gently.

I ran back through the kitchen to the storeroom to grab another case of Lone Star, and my foot slipped on something, and I had to jut my hip out to stay upright. Wendell had just thrown the oily rag from his jeans down on the floor, which of course he had, and I simmered there for a second, until the desire to hurt him moved all the way through and out of me.

I'd never really imagined my life without Wendell. I didn't want to remember the time before him at all—I barely knew that girl. I'd grown up with him there, always there. And he'd never been especially hard to understand, not really. He hadn't ever hurt me except in the little, usual ways people hurt each other. Still, I could smell Doug on the sleeve of my shirt.

Benny was up onstage moving shit around, trying to make more room for Joe, I guessed, even though I was sure it'd all end up right back where it had been, where it always was. And he was checking the left-side mic already, so every minute or so his rasp would cut through the jukebox and the crowd, just a one-two-three at the beginning, but then he started puffing out his cheeks and doing his usual, which was just to say *good goddamn* over and over for the consonants, *good goddamn, good goddamn,* and then laughing like a maniac when people looked up there at him. I hated when he did that. It made the crowd think the music was gonna start earlier than it was, so they'd all rush to the bar at the same time. It messed with the flow, and I was already uneasy, and I knew they wouldn't go on until Joe showed anyway.

I'd lost track of Doug in the thrum of people, but I saw Gwen at a table with Hopper and a couple girls up by the front, near enough I could see the rise of her cheekbones. For a beat I just looked at her. I imagined a woman like that felt looked at all the time, and I felt briefly sorry for her, but just briefly. I turned quick to see if Wendell was looking at her too, and he wasn't, he was serving, but down toward that end of the bar, I could see that Steven was. Looking at her just like I was, I mean, and not hiding it even. She leaned into one of her friends, smiled, took a sip of her drink, and jiggled the rocks.

People were still streaming in, and T.K. had put the brick in front of the door to keep it open. The sun was down for good now. I could smell the thick of the storm coming, but the folks coming in still looked dry and careless. Then I saw Joe just inside the door with a big group of guys, squeezing shoulders as he waded through bodies. His collar up to frame his face and those big rim sunglasses, and yes, he was good, he really was, his songs were better than almost everyone else's, but it was still ridiculous that he got away with being as arrogant as he was. One of the guys behind him was carrying a guitar case awkward and upright, gripping each side like it was heavier than it could've been, a pallbearer trying to usher the body alone. Joe stopped at the table when he saw Gwen and her girls, but the guy kept going past him, set the guitar down smoothly on the front of the stage and then pulled it out to start tuning. I saw a couple boys with them I knew played brass too, and I had no earthly clue how they were all going to fit on the stage together or how the room would handle the noise.

Doug shimmied in from somewhere, waved me over. I grabbed as many beers as I could with both hands and came around the end of the bar to where the girls were sitting. There was a little lull in the sound—the juke was having trouble flipping a record, sounded like—and I could hear without straining for what I thought was probably the last time all night. I heard a clap of thunder and then another one.

"Oh, thank you," Gwen said sweetly when I set down the bottles. "Saved us a trip."

"Deanna," Doug said. "This is my very old friend Joe Ely, wanted you to meet him."

"Hi," I said, and I reached out a wet hand.

Joe turned it in his, then kissed the top of it, and one of the girls let out a laugh that sounded like a donkey braying. He'd been in here a couple times, but he wasn't the kind of guy to go to the bar and get his own drinks.

"I've seen you play," I said, and blushed, trying not to pull my hand back in too fast.

"Of course you have," he said, but Doug looked at me surprised.

"Yeah?" Doug asked.

"Sure."

"Sure, Dougie," Joe said. "She seen me play."

"You ever shut up?" Gwen asked.

"You know I don't, baby," he said. "But I'm real glad you graced us with your presence tonight, I will say."

"When are we going on, Ben?" Doug called up to the stage, but Benny didn't hear him or didn't care. He was bending over his accordion and wiping it gingerly with a rag.

"Better be soon," I heard, and there was Steven again, always there, asking for it.

"Who's this?" Joe asked.

Steven didn't say anything, but he looked at Doug, like he expected Doug to answer for him. Everybody was quiet a beat too long except for finally Hopper, who said, "Joe, meet our friend Steven."

"We met," Steven said. "With Doug at the Armadillo."

"Your friend Steven," Joe said slowly. He pulled his glasses off with a pinch of his fingers, looked Steven up and down with a sort of grimace. "Sure you ain't somebody's kid, Steven? Maybe Dougie's? He's even got your hair, Doug. Smile for me, Steven, let me see those teeth."

"Ha ha ha," Doug said, shuffled his feet a little.

"We met," Steven said again, louder, but Joe had turned away already.

Hopper stood up, gave me a quick look I couldn't quite parse, and moved over toward the stage to say something to Benny, who checked his watch and nodded. "Grab the drinks, let's go," Hop yelled back over at the table, and they started to move.

I left the girls at the table and Steven standing where he was and went back behind the bar to ask Wendell to start prepping for the set. He looked at me and then up toward the stage with a kind of scoff, but he didn't say anything. I sure as hell didn't need it, but I took a quick minute, between serving a big group of good ole boys I'd never seen before and two girls with arms like twigs going at each other about somebody named Noah, and I poured two shots of whatever was closest on the rail. I couldn't keep track of anything in the room, there were so many people. I took one of the shots and then the other. I must've swallowed in between, but I didn't feel it. Doug was checking the front mic, and he looked to Benny for a thumbs-up by the preamp, and then

Joe checked his and glanced over, and Hopper pulled the rag off his snare and folded it in half. Joe tapped his mic again and said, "Come on up," into it, and four more guys, at least, approached the lip of the stage. *No way*, I thought. There was no possible way; the stage was too small. I heard the dull drop-sound of Wendell cutting the power to the juke, and I could see one of Joe's guys talking at Doug and Doug pointing down reluctantly to the floor in front of the stage and shrugging, and that was where they were going to have to play, I saw, and probably pissed as hell, used to twenty extra feet of room.

"Time to move these babes," Benny said into his mic, and Gwen and her friends got up and pulled back and slid the table with them.

I saw Steven try to shift another empty table away from the stage, but he forgot to pull out the chairs first, and one of them crashed backward to the ground.

"He's gonna need a lot of help," Benny said, and the whole room laughed at once, and I saw Doug's face red as a stoplight.

Wendell got up there to shoo Steven away, rearrange. I heard feet stomping in the back and the talk was dying down, and I tried to brace myself, breathe deep, and push hard into the floor with the arches of my feet.

"*Hey*," I heard suddenly. A kid in a yellowed T-shirt so tight I could see the hair on his chest was glaring at me. "Can I get a goddamn beer before this gets going or—"

T.K. closed the front door and cut the lights, and then it was time. They were on.

It was dangerous loud. That first kick and the electrics wailing. The kind of loud that makes you queasy, see dark spots where people should be. Ancient loud, truly, godlike loud. Joe's rasp and two trombones, four mics and the voices in them egging each other on, competing, and a song I didn't know to start the set. And then Joe sat down at the upright, and I'd never heard the piano so wild.

And the rain had started to come down outside too, hard enough after a minute I could hear it hit the tin through the notes. A blast of wind blew the back door open; somebody pulled it closed, and I wished they hadn't. The air in the bar was compressed and thick; Hopper's drums rippled through the soup of it. June storms started and stopped without much warning, and I saw a girl slip through the side door soaked all the way through, her blouse drenched and clingy.

I was back behind the bar, trying to read lips and getting it wrong, but almost everybody just took what I handed them. Bodies were shaking in whatever rhythm Hopper wanted them shaking, and the bass was the roughest heartbeat I'd ever heard, like it belonged to all of us at once, one animal, trapped in a box, cornered and flailing at the walls. I took another shot and then drained half a beer just to feel myself swallow. I just couldn't get comfortable anywhere or anyhow. And then three songs in, Benny picked up the accordion and it bellowed out, and for a split second my body didn't belong to me at all. I felt relieved at my own absence.

"Shit, boys," Joe said into the mic after they crashed back down to earth.

The crowd was screaming, whistling higher and louder till I thought they'd blow. "Hoooooo, baby. I'm dripping. Y'all dripping?" They screamed again. I kept my head down.

"Joe Ely's with us tonight, folks," Doug said. "What you think, Joe?"

"I don't," Joe said.

"Damn right," Benny yelled. "What y'all think, then?" he asked the crowd, and they busted open all over again.

The horns were noodling and Hopper had never stopped with the beat; he was still stomping the kick every two seconds or so. Doug beamed so big it hurt me to look at him, smiling with his whole body like a child, an only child with the world in his hands, or just a grown man on enough uppers and pleasure to forget he's grown.

I wished for the first time all day that I'd stayed sober. Or at least relatively, enough to keep my head from bouncing and careening how it was. I hadn't eaten anything but two bags of Fritos and a few limes soaked in tequila since I'd left the house that morning, but the idea of eating made me feel worse.

It took every bit of strength I had in my body to feel my

way backward into the kitchen. I opened the door for some air, and the rain was tapering off already, but the wind was blowing water out of their puddles in gusts. The door swung a little on its hinges, and I backed up, bent over, and tried to come back to who I was. I clenched through the noise as best I could with my head between my knees until I could stand back up, the ozone puncture of the night and my socks wet in my shoes, the piano keys clicking loud from the stage like a woodpecker and making me crazy. Still, I tried to stay upright, relax my jaw and breathe like I was wading into cold water, slow and methodical, but then a trumpet blast got me right in the throat, and I barely got to the sink before I got sick. I held back my own hair, but my hands were shaky and a couple wet strands fell down around my ears, and when I stopped gagging, I closed my eyes, exhausted, and same as I always did when I was that wrung, I thought about my mother.

After our fourth date in as many nights, I'd come home ready to tell her about Wendell. I wasn't sure I could bring myself to do it. Or to leave her, which was all I wanted to do. But Wendell had driven me up the driveway in the huge Chrysler he had then, over the rutted gravel and the roots of that one pecan jutting up through the ground like a sea creature. I was wearing this dress, I remember, with apples embroidered all over it. I felt like I was playing at being a woman. But then when we pulled up near the porch, Wendell leaned over from the driver's seat, all the way across the bench seat, kissed me, and swallowed up my whole mouth, my whole body, the girl I'd been. He asked what I was going to say, and I felt brave, and I told him I'd just be clear as day, I'd say I met a man.

"I met *somebody,*" he said. "Better that way."

He smiled, and I looked at him and saw him, saw him like I'd see him for the next thirty years—just: there. I swung the door open, slammed it back closed, and climbed up the steps. I smoothed the front of my dress. I'd been gone all day; the sun was setting behind me. I forced myself to turn the knob, and I went in.

The house was completely silent but for the clock in the hallway, ticking away like a soldier. Dust in my nose and hot as an oven, like she hadn't so much as opened a window. I moved slowly, listened for ice clinking in glass in the kitchen, or the wisps of the radio coming down the stairs, but I didn't hear anything besides that clock, 7:27 and 28, 29, 30, 31. I turned into the living room, steadied myself the way I did, for her anger, or her misery, or her eyes.

But I'd gotten none of it. She was just lying there, prone on the floor, her face buried in the old red rug, and her legs half-crumpled up, like at one point they'd been under her. For a moment, a moment as wide and bright as land, I thought she was gone. And when I saw her back lift and fall, I took a big gulp of air and realized I was crying, really sobbing, salt coating my lips and gasping like a baby. She just laid there. The chewed-up nails on her left hand splayed out and calm, the dregs of a handle of gin pooling in the slats of the wood between the couch and the table. I got ahold of myself as best I could, and without thinking bent over to pull her legs straight and slip her shoes off, but I couldn't bring myself to do it. I couldn't bring myself to touch her. I'd already done all I knew to do.

"There you are, shit." I heard Wendell's yell behind me, and I turned.

"It's so loud," I said.

"What?"

"It's too loud," I screamed. The wind blew through the open door. His shirt was untucked, and his blond hair was so wet it looked varnished. He came a couple steps closer.

"I can't hear you," he yelled. "Are you OK?"

I wiped my mouth on my sleeve and moved all the way toward him, grabbed his hands with mine, and held them there between us like we were praying. I kissed the tip of one of his fingers, quick, but it was cold on my lips. And I still don't know why exactly, but I needed so badly to touch him. I pulled his finger into my mouth and sucked on it hard, till it stuck up to the roof, and I swirled soft around the knuckle. I put a flat hand on his stomach and stared right into his eyes and slowed down, let his finger drop down and rest in a pocket of heat on my tongue. But he looked at me like he'd never seen me before, like he'd come in looking for his wife and found instead a completely different woman.

Then the light flickered, quick. Wendell's forehead creased with worry, and he pulled back his hand and looked up at the bulb above the sink. I was empty, needy.

"You still love me?" I asked, barely.

"What?" he yelled.

"Do you love me?" I yelled, but it wasn't what I meant to ask even. Love wasn't the problem. It was just an easy name for a feeling that doesn't have one.

"Of course I do," he said.

The lights flickered off and back on again, all of them.

"Oh, fuck," he said.

It wasn't more than fifteen seconds then, the chorus of a punched-up Flatlanders song burning and rolling and the bass stepping and the crowd's noise cresting and foaming, until a big crack like wood splitting, and the power blew. The light above me and Wendell, and all the rest of them, went dark.

It didn't take but three minutes for Wendell to flip off the breaker, rejig something in the circuit box, and flip the breaker back on, but it was plenty long. It was black and quiet but for the wind. The sudden silence was scary, feverish—it was somehow twice as loud as the music had been. By the time I felt my way back to behind the bar, people were starting to grind and scream, push into and against each other. I smacked into something—one of the barbacks—and stepped on her foot; I heard her yelp. Then the snap of a pool ball hitting the ground. I could hear Joe's voice, whining, really going, about his gear and couldn't see shit, and *the living fuck, barely through the set, half—*

My eyes adjusted some, and I could see by the cherries of people's smokes and what gray light seeped in through the door people had pushed open that they were just waiting, mostly, standing in place like pent livestock, no longer totally in charge of themselves. There were clusters of bodies in the doorframes, but I could only see glimpses of faces, flashes of eyes in the quick blaze of cigarette lighters. The crowd sizzled. The night had become something enormous all at once, and the room was smoldering hot, hotter for the darkness.

"Just hang on, y'all," I heard T.K. yell over the din, and on his way out the front.

I saw people follow him out through the doorway. Not for the first time I wished we'd put in some damn windows when we'd redone the place.

"Wendell," I heard Doug yell, and Benny screamed, "Can we please God fix this right fucking now?" and a clatter from the wall behind the stage I thought was probably Hopper's stool falling over when he stood up. One of the trumpets blasted a high note suddenly, and the whole crowd jumped and squealed, and a wave of pure hatred for whichever guy thought that'd be funny in this moment rose up like acid from my stomach and burned. I heard a glass fall and shatter.

"Wendell," Doug yelled again.

"He's got it," I said, but too soft.

"Get off me, you prick," I heard a girl's voice say, somewhere close to me, and somebody else laughed.

"Jesus Christ, what's the deal?" Benny screamed.

"He's on it!" I yelled this time.

"He's on it," somebody repeated.

"He's on it," I heard again, loud, and I knew from the pitch of the voice and the desperation it was Steven. God, there was something about everything he did, that kid. He couldn't have possibly made it harder to like him, even in the dark. I felt a fresh flood of disgust I wasn't sure I could countenance without it sending me back to the kitchen sink. The strength of it surprised me.

"Get *off* me," I heard the girl say again, and a slapping sound.

"Goddamn hippie smell anyway."

The bar started whirring first, the water lines picked back up, and then the stage lights flashed, once, twice, and on, so I could see Benny bending over the instruments. A big boom from one of the amps getting juiced all at once, and people jumped again. Doug looked out at the crowd, grimaced, and then turned to the bar and saw me.

He was mortified, I could tell. He looked small, young. I'd never seen Doug so deflated, not once. I'd never been able to see through his pose the way I could now. Up there onstage, in the glow circle of the spotlight, his face was beet red. His shoulders slumped under a pressure so heavy I thought he might buckle. He looked like he might say something to the crowd, and I held my breath. The room was still bulging and pulsing, but before Doug opened his mouth, somebody thought to reach over and hit the floor lights by the front door.

The whole bar lit up then. People looked sickly in the sudden fluorescent light, washed out and ragged. Their stretched, sweaty faces and a dirty sombrero some guy had on perched high on his head like a dead flag. Even the girls looked haggard, routed. They turned away from the stage and toward each other in their little clutches. Doug wasn't going to say anything after all. He hiked his jeans up by the belt loops and knelt down over his guitar.

"Shit," Hopper said. "OK."

"Can we check the guitars?" Doug asked. "I'm scared the Tele's fucked."

"Mine's fine," Benny said.

"This amp shorted out," Joe said, like somebody'd killed his dog.

Doug was quiet.

"It's fine, we'll get the other one," Hopper said.

"It shorted, it's fucking done."

"We got an extra."

"Some ragtag shit you got out here, Dougie," Joe said, and snarled how he did.

And then Hopper was in front of me with his eyes flashing. I went to pour him a shot, but he grabbed the bottle off the bar while I hunted a glass and just bombed it straight. A blonde next to him I'd never seen got up on her tiptoes and nuzzled his shoulder.

People were starting to migrate. Hop brushed off the girl, mildly, like you would a fly, rushed back to the stage, and flipped the switch on the front mic, then off and then back on again: a screech of feedback and a lowing whine.

"Give us ten minutes, people, fifteen," he said into it, and some boy in the back yelled, "Take your time, baby."

The room was clearing out little by little, but people were coming up to get drinks to take outside. Christ, nobody was really going to leave. Time moves funny around here sometimes: months can pass like hours, and a single, big night can last a year. Nobody walks away from a night like that, I mean. And the tail of the storm had to be whipping its way east by now, and the wind'd be dying down. The roles felt flipped— the band had lost control, and the crowd had reached down and picked it up. Who wouldn't want to stick around for the rest of that feeling? I saw T.K. come back through the front door with a smoke in his lip and adjust the lights until it wasn't so ghostly and awful anymore, and voices kept whistling and buzzing.

"Don't go anywhere," I heard a voice yell from the front, Steven again.

Wendell came up behind me, and I turned. He said, "We're good," but after a quick nod, he left again, toward the stage to help sort out what needed sorting. I saw Steven's greasy head up there too, shimmering and bouncing; the kid was a pinball. I filled a pint glass with water from the back tap, and I followed Wendell carefully, not quite steady on my feet. The drunk was mostly gone, and my body felt wrung-out, busted.

"Janky-ass shit," Joe was saying to nobody in particular.

"God, you're whiny as ever," Gwen said back to him, teasing a straw around the corner of her mouth the whole time. "Be a man about it, you never lost power in your life or what?"

Doug gave her a pleading look like *God, don't,* but also: *Thank you.* Steven snickered, and for a split second I was worried Joe might kick his face in, right there from the stage.

"So glad you're here," he said to Gwen instead, "always a pleasure."

"What y'all need?" Wendell asked. Even on the floor his head was almost level with the front mic.

"A better bar, for one," Joe said.

Doug looked like he was gonna faint with shame, and he busied himself adjusting a cable. I saw Gwen reach an easy hand out toward Wendell as if to apologize for Joe, and then pull it back, and even I could see it wasn't more than friendly, but my insides pulsed anyway like they were getting blended. I looked for some lean from Wendell but saw none. I took a slow sip of water and swished it around my mouth.

"OK, OK, OK," Doug said. "Well, we need the amp from the gear in the back."

"I'll get it," Steven said.

"No, you won't," Wendell said, and he made toward the closet.

"Damn, just tryin' to help, friendo," Steven said, and then he did this little move, this weird half jig at Wendell's back, the oddest thing. A skip of his feet and a flick of his neck. He sniffled, and I could see the bloodred of his eyes in the stage light. He was a real clown, a wasted little puppet.

"Hey, you OK?" Doug asked him, quick and quiet, like he couldn't help it.

"Excellent," Steven said, beaming.

"God," Benny said, a smoke between his fingers.

"You ain't gotta be nice to everybody, Dougie," Joe said.

"No shit, thank you," Benny said.

Wendell was back with the amp, and he set it down right in front of Joe, who looked at it like it disgusted him. He slid off the stage.

"Going outside to cool down," Joe said.

Benny and Hopper moved to follow him, and Steven said, "Be right out," and Joe laughed.

"I fucking know," Benny said.

"You're something else, aren't you?" Joe said, and for a second got up close to Steven's face.

Steven shifted his weight back, but he didn't look surprised or any smaller than he usually did.

"I am," Steven said. "Sure."

"Leave him alone, Joe," Hopper said.

"Everybody already likes you, Hopper, you can stop trying so hard," Joe said, but he was still staring at the kid. "How'd you get this way?" he asked, almost conspiratorial, like he really did want an answer. Steven looked up at Doug, who didn't say anything at all.

"We're all fucking weirdos, anyway," Gwen said, and then something that sounded like *je swee da tro*. She was sitting down in a chair but no table, rolling a smoke in her lap, a tight little thing, licking the paper real slow.

"I'm sorry, what?" Benny said, and coughed up a laugh.

"It's Sartre," she said. "French."

"Nah, we're not though," said Joe. "Not like him. You know what they say about strays."

"What do they say?" Benny asked.

Joe got up real close to Steven then, took a step in so Steven staggered back, threw an arm toward the stage, and caught himself. Joe pulled a Zippo from his vest pocket, flicked the flint right in Steven's eyes. "Oh, you know, just that you can feed 'em if you have to, but don't you dare let 'em in the house."

"Too late," Steven said, and goddamn the kid, he grinned.

Doug came up to the bar. He was watching Joe walk toward the front door, and he walked right into the wood in front of Wendell.

"Should I turn on the box?" Wendell asked.

"No," Doug said, "Joe just needs a quick break."

"Yeah, he does," Wendell said. "I can't do shit about the power shorting."

"I know," Doug said softly.

"I really can't do shit. Y'all know you have a damn circus plugged into the wall. You can tell them that."

"Don't worry about Joe; he'll brush it off."

"I'm not worried about anybody in this place, to tell you the truth," Wendell said. "Y'all are welcome to go play somewhere else if you want to."

He waited a second for Doug to respond. Looking at Doug was like looking at a fresh brushfire crackling; stand in his wind and he might die, come too close and he might send out an angry spark to remind you he was burning, leave you a scar. Wendell kinda tilted his head in my direction and he walked away.

"Can I just get a beer?" Doug asked me.

I reached down into the trough and handed Doug a Pearl, and his pinky brushed my palm when he took the can from my hand. He drained it in four gulps, barely closed his throat between, and I watched his Adam's apple jerk and fall with it. I grabbed another one, set it in front of him, and saw the wet of it slink down toward the wood. I was still sipping at my water, trying to calm my stomach, fill the hole left by the old, hot liquor. Over Doug's shoulder I saw Steven sitting, alone it seemed, at a table on the far side of the room, and not even with his back to the wall but to the people instead, like nobody else would sit in a crowd. Anybody in the world could've come up behind him, I mean. I hoped with my whole heart he stayed right where he was.

I poured two big shots of the shine I kept around, the bottle so foggy I felt like an old crone, or a cowboy, when I held it. I took the smallest little sip I could manage off the top of mine and remembered immediately why I rarely pulled it out. Doug took his without saying a word, and I watched it smack him.

"You OK?" I asked.

"No," he said, head down.

"Sorry about the power," I said.

"Yeah," he said.

"Nobody's fault," I said.

"OK," he said.

"OK?" I asked.

"OK," he said, exhaled. "It's nobody's fault."

I was exhausted. I didn't feel like I had any tenderness left to give. I wanted to be alone. I didn't want to be in the bar anymore. I didn't want to be anywhere else I could picture either.

"I'm trying, Deanna," he said.

"You're trying to what?"

"I didn't say a thing about it, did I?" he said.

"What are you trying?" I asked.

A girl I'd never seen with bright, wet eyes skated in beside him, asked for change for a five for the cigarette machine, reached out and ran a hand down Doug's sleeve. I practically spat the bills into her hand.

"We can call it if you want," I said to him when she'd left.

"Huh?"

"If you're done."

"We're not fucking done," he said. "We can't be. I have to get it right tonight."

"'Cause of Joe?"

"Yeah," he said. "It matters."

"What matters?" I tried to keep easy, but the conversation felt like walking in the woods at night, pitfalls everywhere. I needed another body to guide me through it.

"Tonight. Joe. Everything. I don't think I have that many chances left, and he really likes the new stuff, he really does. I need this to work, Dee. I need something to change. And I—nah, I don't want to jinx it," he said. "If we haven't already."

"I'm sorry," I said.

"Nobody's fault," he said. "Nobody's fault," again, slow and deliberate, and I swear to God I thought he might cry then. When he looked up at me, I felt seized, and I cataloged every bit of my body he could see above the bar, straightened my neck and forced my shoulder blades down my back.

"Hey," I said gently, and inclined toward him a little but not too far, like you would a feral kitten you didn't want to spook. "*Are* you good?"

"What's good anyway?" he asked. "I have no idea. I guess I'm still here?" He sounded like he might actually be asking. "I have to go out there and convince him to come back in. We gotta get back on."

"Whenever you're ready," I said. I'd go out with him and tell T.K. to help herd.

"It's too much for me tonight, Dee," he said. "All these people and Joe here, and I barely have it in me to try anymore."

"I get it."

"No," he said. "I'm really worn. I'm just worn out."

Keep going, I thought. *Keep going. Get the hell out while you can still get out. Before your life solidifies around you and all you have left to look at are the walls.*

His hand drummed a slow beat on the bar, stopped.

"Sometimes you just gotta tell people what you need," I said.

"What if I don't know what I need? Or it's too much to ask for? And what if I can't, you know, get it?"

I reached over the wood of the bar and laid my palm down on top of Doug's knuckles. Over his shoulder, I saw Steven bent over at the waist, sucking up whatever he'd lined up on the table. Doug spun a finger up and over mine and rubbed my nail like he was worrying a prayer bead. Next to two empty cans and a rag wet with booze and the tip jar half full of nickels, he opened his eyes a sliver. His eyelashes glittered in the light. I would've stayed there for the rest of my days, let the earth go on spinning around us and the doors swinging open and closed against the bricks, still as dead and right there with him in the good God middle of the world.

"What do you need?" I asked. "Really." But he slipped his hand out from underneath mine and ran it through the part in his hair.

"One more beer. Just one more, I think," he said, like I couldn't have possibly meant anything more than that.

The band wanted it dark again. Benny had asked Wendell to cut the lights completely, including the stage lights, so all we had on was the track lighting around edges of the ceiling. In the charcoal of the room, faces were just broad shadows, and the noise, with almost everybody back inside now, was impatient. I thought it was likely too late to get back to the thrill of the set before the power cut, but I would've been a goddamn fool to underestimate the kind of rapture Doug could summon.

The horns were back in their makeshift pit, shuffling their feet. Doug and Joe and Benny and Tulsa with his bass hiked up into his armpits like he was sitting on the toilet. Doug's guitar hung limp off his shoulders. Everybody coffin-still at their mics and Hopper back there at his set like a mural on the side of a building, wind-worn and faded. Even the kids bellied up to the bar had forgotten to order, had turned their backs to lean against the wood or perch on stools, and they waited.

"We're gonna try this one more time," Doug said, and the crowd cheered loud and steady, like they were going to scream all the way into the first tune. But fifteen seconds passed; thirty. The band was silent. The crowd stood still and surged at the same time. I can't explain the feeling of a room like that: it's wild and primal, bigger than my own body or anybody else's. Sometimes the only way people can ever be together, I think, truly together, is in a crowd like that.

T.K. hit the spot, and the whole stage was bleached with light. Hopper beamed the way he does, kindly. He grinned like he was just delighted by every person in the place, like he'd never been up there before. His foot dropped. The slowest, cleanest beat I'd ever heard pounded into every tiny space in the room. Just the big bass and the silence between it, no cymbals or anything, his hands cold on his knees. It was startlingly heavy. I heard a moan. The beat knock, knock, knocking off the walls. Hopper could've brought down the ceiling on top of all these people, and they would've thanked him from under the rubble.

Doug swept his hair out of his face. Benny whipped his guitar across his body, and the cord jerked like a leash behind a loose dog. He came in with the riff, the melody stair-stepping, but slow, simple, no keening or dressing or anything. It was "Walk Softly on This Heart of Mine," but I'd never heard it like this. It was my favorite of everything they did, which I felt a little guilty about, because it wasn't one of Doug's songs, and it was really, when you got down to it, just an old country song. Such a simple little song, I mean. Just three chords, coming home.

Benny's guitar went silent again. And still the bass drum churning, over and over again. Doug as calm as I'd seen him all night at the stand. Benny's hands perched on the neck of the Telecaster, lingering. How long could they push it? I wasn't sure how much more the room could withstand. And Hopper just kept going. But when Doug finally, finally whispered that first word, Benny's high strings vibrated, and the horns came in from underneath, I felt a rush of adrenaline. My fingers burned, and my lips were bitter. *You.* It was a rush of water in a dry river; a needle slipping through the skin. The crowd thrashed open.

It sounded busier toward the front door though than near the stage. Or it all sounded the same, but the back of the crowd was moving more frenzied, crashing against each other. I could hear the faint cottoned smack of bodies. The front door was closed, and T.K. was somewhere else, and the crowd was so big I had to wait for people to dance out of the way to see through; it was like trying to look through a pack of animals. Under an arm, over a shoulder. I glanced at Wendell, and I knew he could see it too, because he was looking back at the crowd while he rinsed a rocks glass under the water tap; it had filled and the water was pouring out of it like a pitcher. Then I heard something hit the floor.

I saw Wendell make a move, but by the time he'd even gotten to the bar door, I saw Steven lifted up in the air, hoisted by his armpits. He had a dark, wet stain on his chest. I watched a big, big man throw a meaty hook and knock Steven's head clear back into the chest of whoever was holding him. Then he dropped again, momentarily free.

"Stop," I croaked.

But the sound, still. Benny was playing the piano now, standing up, pounding the keys like they'd gone at his sister. Joe singing the chorus, *love love*, and my heart in my throat. Gwen dancing with her girls. A flash of pale skin.

"Wendell," I said louder, but it was Doug who looked at me from the stage. He was still playing, and singing, but the turn of his mouth told me he could see more than I could. He looked back down at his guitar.

I trailed Wendell, limboed under the bar but banged the top of my head hard enough to make my eyes water. Still, I started to swim through the crowd toward the corner. Elbows in, shuffling my feet, trying to avoid lit cigarettes. I felt carried too, I mean, clumsily and reluctantly. I kept my eyes on Wendell. Steven surfaced again, near the back wall, but I could only catch a glimpse of him, his hair matted to his scalp.

I waited for the drums to stutter, even for a second, but they didn't. I waited for Doug to stop, to say something, but he didn't either. Joe was barreling into the bridge. I listened to the music from where I was stuck in a thicket of arms, and they were still going at him, the poor dumb kid. Wendell fought through the din ahead of me.

"Touch me again," I heard somebody say. I wiped a gloss of sweat off my arms, and then I rubbed my palms fast and hard on the thighs of my jeans, flexed my wrists.

"Do that again, boy," and I saw a thick, balding guy holding a beer in one of his hands. He bent over, and something came out of his mouth in a stream. The man took a swig of his Lone Star and dumped the rest out right where he'd spit.

Wendell emerged, clamping Steven out in front of him with both huge hands, awkward, like a man without a baby holds one. The kid looked so bad I was surprised he was still awake. A mucky slobber dripped off his forehead, and one of his eyes was sinking into his face like a button, but when he saw me he said, "Dee, hey," hoarse but generous, like we could've been running into each other in the produce section or at the pool. The song was just lasting forever, longer than they ever let it go, and when I looked back up at the stage, Doug was playing with his back to the crowd. I saw him make a swirling move with his hand, the go again motion, and they started into the chorus again. Wendell was taking Steven toward the door, and from where I was following I saw Steven crane his neck around Wendell's middle, wince, and look back at the stage. People around me exhaled as we passed, and the crowd coagulated and filled our wake fast as rushing water.

"Good riddance," somebody near me said, and it sounded breathy, like a woman's voice, but I couldn't trace it back to a face.

"Is he OK?" a guy asked when I moved past, had to yell some. He couldn't have been more than twenty, big nose and black glasses and a full white three-piece suit he was soaking right through—I could smell him. And I wondered what town he'd come from, and if this one would give him whatever he was looking for, and if he'd stay here forever.

167

CALLIE COLLINS

I came up to the door behind Wendell, who'd jerked it open and kicked the brick over to hold it, put Steven down right in the doorway, and pushed him through. Steven had crumpled onto the dirty ground, and I knew mud had to be soaking through the back of his overalls. He looked up at Wendell and pulled himself up to sitting, but his legs still twisted under him unruly, in a way I really, really didn't want to see.

"Thank you, Wendell," he said slow, searching Wendell's face. "Thanks."

"Get out," Wendell said, and he moved toward Steven, who flinched and tried to scoot farther back. I stood still, buzzing and staring at the lines in Wendell's red plaid, the golds and grays you couldn't see from afar.

"It really wasn't, I didn't—"

"Go home," Wendell said.

"Yeah, just need a second but I'm fine, all good. Fine."

"I didn't ask," Wendell said. "Just go home, Jesus Christ." He slid past me and left the two of us there alone.

"Amen," Steven said, still on the dirt. He half laughed to himself, and I wanted to hug him, or kick him harder than I'd ever kicked anything. He didn't seem scared, and I wanted him to. I pulled a bandana out of my back pocket—it was cleanish—and I tossed it to him, watched it fall into his neck. He grabbed it and pressed it up against the back of his head.

"Be right back in," he said. "'Preciate y'all looking out."

"Steven," I said, "please just go. It's over for tonight. Get yourself home."

"No way, baby, ain't over till . . ." He trailed off, opened his mouth, and tested a tooth with the tip of a finger, wiggled, to see if it was still in tight enough to stay.

"Steven," I said.

"Ma'am," he said.

I looked at him broken there one last time, took two steps backward, nudged the brick away with my toe, and watched the door float closed between us.

THREE

Steven's God is a Hick God. Once upon a time, deep in the small attic of his mind, Steven gave his God a face. It was the kind of thing he just did, and long before he knew he'd done it. Steven gave his God a few good pockmarks on the cheeks and a jaw hard as chiseled ice, plenty sexy enough even then, to run a tongue along. And Steven gave his God a voice too. Sure. The voice came easy. No room for that stodgy King James—Steven would have none of that hitherto-shalt-thou—in a world already cold and confusing enough. He gave Hick God a good uncle's drawl instead, yes, scent of East Texas pine and rolling.

They ain't talked in a while, Steven and his Hick God. Not till recent. Steven does perfectly fine without. But Steven's beat again, barely got himself off the ground and around the wall of the bar to a folding chair by the pallets, a leg sunk far in the mud so it pitched him forward, and a little puddle of rain in the seat soaking through his denim. He fingers a sopping bandana. *Hick God, Hick God,* Steven thinks, and he can hear Him murmuring back, sweet, breeze-like. Steven's face feels broken pure in half. His hands are numb.

I do love you, Hick God, Steven thinks.

I love you too, baby, he hears Hick God say. *Wipe your face,* He says, and Steven does, but not gentle enough. Not nearly. Something inside Steven's body knows trouble even when Steven himself has no damn clue, so here comes Hick God for the trouble.

Steven knows from trouble, Lord, and this ain't it. Not big-time trouble, anyway.

Boy, were that true, says Hick God.

Were that ever once true, He says, *we'd both be someplace else.*

Steven tries to smile, even though it hurts like a mother-fucker. Hick God embarrasses Steven, but Steven knows He can still make magic if He wants. Steven's pretty sure he embarrasses Hick God too, but He can still turn the night around, if He decides to. It's still early. No sadness or thump in the gut lasts forever—Steven's busted body and racing veins and stupor despite.

Steven can still hear the guitars meanwhile, yelping out the doorjambs and slithering through the cracks in the walls. Hopper's drums wet-clap the ground. Steven slips off his shoes, kicks 'em back under the chair, and plants his feet in the earth as far as hard can push them. He wants a rhythm outside his own. He wants to feel like a child. He wants to be soothed, wiped, sung a lullaby. He wants Hick God to stick around a good minute if He would. Oh, He sure would. *Good of you to ask.* Wet gravel scurries up like friendly bugs in between every single one of Steven's toes.

S teven's hit with a plump bloom of sound, and then it's gone just as quick: the door, maybe the front one. He smells skunk, hears voices like airwave static beneath the music, readies himself to nod hello, but nobody comes around the corner. He drops his head into his hands, but that makes him queasy. Queasier. He pulls back up.

Lemme look, then, says Hick God.

Steven's left cheek is cratered, a bone fidgeting loose. He can't hear very well. The world slides in and out of tune: sharp, cloying. His eyes feel lost. They click and stall in their sockets. His chest—is there still a chest under there? His legs are there, but only faintly. Gashes tear his scalp and his neck, sticky and juicy. His heart is stuttering, a snare on a roll.

Come on now. You don't gotta do that, Hick God, thinks Steven. *You don't gotta list it out.* Like Steven's a collection of parts. Steven's a man. And doesn't Steven know his own body well enough without You here to catalog it? This is exactly why he never wants You around. Steven tastes metal on his lips, licks it swirly off. He's going back inside in a minute or two, three. He vibrates a little, pulsates, but he's fine.

Steven looks up. He scans the dark for a face besides Hick God's, but there's not a one. They're out here alone, just the two of them, together in a rolling, erupting ocean of black, and then almost-black, and then gray, and then moon-colored, burnished. Steven keeps his eyes open while they adjust, keeps them open until he can see again.

W hat do you see, baby?

Oh Lord, don't pretend You don't know. Steven sees all the old shame. He sees the same humiliation he's worked so hard to leave behind him. When he was young, that shame felt as big as a house and just as desolate, and now it builds itself up brick by brick right out of the dirt in front of Steven. He sees it rise up in the distance, across the lot, past all the trees and the cars. It doesn't look altogether terrible now. It beckons him almost, with those big windows warm and wide, and Steven needs to sober up a little. But he's going back inside. He's going back in a minute.

Tell you what, says Hick God. *I wish we could talk in the morning. When the sun's up. Every once in a while.*

I got kicked out of mornings, Steven thinks.

You got kicked out of the Second Avenue Baptist Church of Corsicana, Texas. Had zip to do with me.

Whatever, Steven says. *You never take responsibility for anything. And it was morning all the same.* Steven can't stand the mornings, goes to bed as late as he can to sleep right on through them. Yeah, he got kicked out of church, between the adoration and the intercession, but then he also got kicked out of his family, and kicked out of the county really, felt like. Steven got kicked out of everything he knew between breakfast and lunch. He can still feel the soles on him. Steven hates mornings.

But mornings are great! says Hick God. *With a cup of coffee and a clear head and a nice little cake doughnut, even.*

et's go, *Hick God*. Steven needs suddenly to move. Steven's gotta get up and off this chair. Steven wants this part of the night to be over. Steven wants to dance. He can hear Doug's voice now too, starting up a new tune, and he wants to hold on to the sound of the verse like it's a rope line, shimmy right along it and kick Hick God somewhere it hurts.

No use blaming me for any of it, says Hick God. *And anyway, you did suck off the preacher's boy in the choir loft during "Be Thou My Vision," did you not?*

Steven can't help it: he laughs so hard and loud he makes Hick God giggle too. It feels sacred to laugh together like that, with Hick God. It's a true moment of holy, out here in the night. It's miraculous, a miracle.

Steven does know a miracle when a miracle comes. He doesn't need Hick God for that. Steven's seen heaven before, he has. He knows heaven better than a lot of people, *fuck you*, and he's only nineteen. Heaven was up in that loft. Mercer's hand on the back of Steven's head, pushing in time with the prayer. Steven could hear Mercer's new deep voice, promising obedience, felt the beat thrum hard in Steven's own mouth. That one ecstatic shudder of Mercer's knee. They wouldn't have even been up there if they hadn't been borrowing the Episcopal church while they reroofed Second Avenue. Baptists don't believe in choir lofts. Heaven was that handful of seconds anyway, before he peeked around Mercer's hip and saw the deacon.

Heaven was the first time he saw Doug play. He'd gone out with his roommate one night a few months ago, in the winter, a couple weeks after he'd moved into the house. Night came early in January and Steven was still broken up about that guy Henry, who'd been on Steven's shift, checking meters up by the capitol one Wednesday afternoon, had taken Steven home with him, and then booted Steven before dinner.

"Just fake it, you'll feel better," his roommate said, scratched at a sideburn. "Act happy, be happy."

So Steven went out, and thank God he did. That was the best advice Steven had ever gotten. He walked into the 'Dillo, through the beer garden for the first time and in through the doors, and he smacked right into a new dream.

Doug played the guitar like he was sitting a wild horse; it bucked under his hands and he let it. He looked like an angel up on that stage, and Steven changed. He started to move a little, and the music taught him how to dance, and he thought he could feel everything he'd been before—all he was, all he'd ever prayed to be, and all he'd hated he wasn't— slough right off, a dead skin of Steven. That was heaven, had to be. Steven, dissolving.

All he'd done tonight was start to dance. He just fell into somebody. He was slipping and grooving, clicking with the tom, normal stuff, in the back of the crowd. Everybody else was moving too. The room was dark and sparking. And he only lost his footing for a second, and then to get himself back upright, he accidentally grazed the man in front of him, the guy's mid-back. Steven's hand sledded down the hard muscle. He didn't even try to hold on—knew better than that—but without the help he stumbled again. He tried to right himself without using his hands, but he overcorrected and slipped backward into another man, felt a hard chest against his shoulder and a rush in his head. Even still, Steven thought the palms he felt close around his hips might be helpful—or wanting, even—but no, of course they weren't. They hardened, clawed. They spun him around and it was over before it'd even begun. Steven went as limp as he could and waited for the song to stop. He waited for somebody to come.

Steven's problem with heaven is that it leaves, Hick God. It always leaves him. Deacon Wade had grinned down at him there on his knees, repulsed and thrilled. Mercer zipped his fly fast as he could and skulked away, tiptoed down the spiral stairs, and Steven was left to hold it all alone. He walked home from the service the longest way he could find—quiet through the alleys, sweating through his Sunday clothes— and then he hid behind a brick column on the front porch while he thought through all the possible words he could say. He hadn't needed them anyway. Word of Steven had traveled faster than Steven. The front room was empty, and all his clothes were folded into two paper bags and set down by the dark fireplace. Two hundred and twenty dollars paperclipped to the top of one and no note at all.

Heaven never stays long enough to catch, and it leaves faster when he tries, and Steven can't keep himself from trying. He tries to tame heaven, subdue it. He clutches the reins of it until they cut through his palms. He crushes the delicate life right out. Steven's always trying. Steven tries so hard he wishes he'd never known heaven in the first place, and he doesn't want to talk about it anymore, but Steven has seen heaven. He has.

Son, Hick God sighs. *You really haven't.*

*G*et up, Steven, move it if you're gonna move. Stomp those *feetsies on the ground.* He would, Hick God—he wants to. If only it were a little easier. If only Steven weren't so drunk his very cells are sludgy, if only he weren't so high he's sitting even when he's standing, if only Steven weren't Steven. But Steven is always Steven. Steven never gets what he asks for.

I ain't a wishing well, baby, says Hick God. *You know that's not how I do.*

But Steven needs so little. All he's asking for is a little lift, a shoulder, some strength now to stand. He couldn't ask for any less. And Steven talks to Hick God, doesn't he? He's out here talking, even though the talking hurts. He asked Hick God to stay, even. He says the goddamn prayers. He can't sleep if he doesn't pray first—trust him, he's tried. He might not want to believe in You, Hick God, fine. But he does any-way, and You well know it. Steven feels You, all the time. He believes. He suffers through all the extra, useless pain that comes with believing. Lord Almighty, just help him up.

Hick God's given Steven some good, it's true. The hymns he still loves. They were the only music kid Steven was allowed. The best ones thundered and broke open on top of him. Even the boring ones were better than nothing. He'd asked his father once why the pastor didn't sing the sermons too; it would've been easier to care. Papa laughed in his guilty way: its own kind of music. Steven would drive all the way to the store on the west side for groceries so he could idle in the lot with the windows down and catch snatches of KSCS out of the cars that picked it up from Dallas. Steven learned the sound of round piano octaves and the clean twang of the acoustic too, but never in his whole life could he have dreamed up a Telecaster.

But what else, Hick God? Gave Steven a father in bed, disfigured in the legs from a car wreck before Steven was born, frozen and cowed and he never stood again. Hick God gave Steven a mother too. Acolyte of You, Hick God, all-the-way-in disciple, a particularly normal kind of cruel. Steven mostly remembers her pushing Papa's wheelchair down the aisle, past the faces in the pews and right on through their sniveling. She'd been the one who'd really seen Steven, had hated him for it, and he knew it, even though she'd never once talked straight about it. Yeah, she'd read to him Leviticus while she cooked his peas. She'd warned him before she said good night about Matthew's road to evil—broad and one-way, she said—like the devil was gonna sneak in and coax him out of his blankets. She'd looked at Steven like she could already see his taillights.

That's enough about that. That's enough. *Nobody's perfect, bub. Everybody's got their own sins to try and swallow.* Guess that's true, Hick God. But in Steven's experience, sins go down a lot easier if You savor them some, chew on 'em a while. Just gotta wring out all the flavor, and then whooooosh, Lord. Right down the hatch.

Y ou know, come to think of it, Steven's got a pint of Jack in the truck. He's standing now. He's stumbling toward the spot he's pretty sure the truck is moored. His bare feet burn, too soft for carrying his weight, even though he feels much lighter than he knows he is. Steven's floating. He needs a drink for ballast, to settle him back down. A couple pills too, maybe, take the edge off the coke—he'd snuck an extra baggie of something off George's dresser. George wouldn't miss them, whatever they were. He works at a pharmacy and is generous with it. *Too generous*. He keeps Steven in company, at least, which is way more than Steven can say for Hick God.

Steven sees what he thinks is the foamy green of the Datsun in the moonlight. It's under a tree he doesn't remember. Walks around the right and isn't sure until he opens the door that it belongs to him. He smiles a grateful smile. He swings himself into the passenger side and squeezes the handle of the glove box till it drops open, leans his head back against the rest and forgets what he's meant to do until he feels the glass of the pint in his palm. It's lukewarm from the heat and goes down like water.

S teven spots a group of ghosts in the side mirror, under the floodlight by the wall, while he's dry swallowing the chalky tabs he picked out of the plastic. He rips a nail over the seal of the empty bag, drops it on the floorboard. They're mostly girls—Steven can tell, even from here, by the way they move. He cleans his throat with another gulp of whiskey, hiccups accidentally and loud—his whole throat shudders and burns, like it might send everything back up.

Steven feels watched. By Hick God always, but also by whoever's out there, by the little red eyes of their smokes, by the trees and the trucks. He slides down on the bench seat to wait and breathes real shallow. He rests his head on the driver's side and looks up at the gear shift. He closes his eyes for a minute or two, maybe longer, but he pries them open again and peeps up over the back of the seat like a prairie dog. The people have scattered, and Steven is lonesome again.

*O*nly one fix for lonesome, baby, and the fix is in, says Hick God. *The fix came all the way up here even. You're bleeding again.*

Steven feels around and finds a split at the back of his head, fishes out a piece of pebble dipped inside. *Prove it, then,* Steven tells Hick God, and he looks at the tiny rock chip in his hand, a pearl. Give Steven a fix. Give Steven a sign. Give Steven a dry towel. Give Steven a cold beer. Give Steven a steady rhythm. Give Steven some real love, loud love, love he can point to and touch. Give Steven a real home, or at least let him keep this one.

Steven's tired now. He's too heavy in this truck; it's sinking fast under his weight. He can feel the tires digging through the clay and the roots underneath them, and he can feel a scary sort of rumbling underneath the roots, and he can feel some dark abyss underneath that, and he doesn't know if he trusts Hick God to keep him from falling down into it.

B *uck up, son. Try and think of something pretty.*
Fine. Had Hick God been there last night? Late,
Steven means, with Doug.

Sure.

Is Steven remembering it right or wrong?

What you remember?

Real sad songs, but Steven was hopeful anyway. The girls
had gone out front to get some air, and the guys had finally
followed. Benny had slapped Steven's back on his way to grab
another beer like he was being friendly, but he wasn't, he
never was, and it stung. Only a couple lights were still on, the
kitchen door closed and Dee and Wendell were long gone.
Hopper was the last to wander outside, with a joint closed up
in his hand and shuffling his feet. Steven could hear them
all outside, soft-howling, kicking the dirt around. Thought
Doug would get up too, but he stayed at the table, and Steven
couldn't believe his luck.

The look that had furled itself open over Doug's face while
he dug for a butt in the ashtray. The deep-down blues, pret-
tiest thing Steven had ever seen, lifted up Doug's cheekbones

and softened his temples. Steven had asked about You, didn't even mean to but needed something to say. Doug said the only God he believed in was called B-flat. Church of music, brother. Sounded so nice to Steven he thought he might fall out of his chair, and he let Doug keep talking. Steven gulped. He shook, but only a little. He cut another two lines on the table for something to do with his hands. He lit a smoke as deliberate as he could, prayed Doug would look at his mouth. Had looked, yes, Steven thinks he did. Doug started talking faster then, about who even knows? Steven was barely listening. He was staring at Doug's forearms on the table. He touched one. And when Doug kept on talking anyway, Steven held on and on and on.

Steven's going back inside now. He can still catch the tail end of the first set. He'll keep his hips still. He'll be nice to Wendell, push his fingers into his eyes until he sees red and then his eyes will rim and look sorry. He'll watch from the back, just follow the guitar, watch the big burn of it, until Steven can imagine he is himself the guitar. He'll find Doug when they're done.

Steven braces himself, nudges open the door with the side of a foot, swings his legs out the opening. He slips what's left of the whiskey into his front pocket so the glass snuggles right into Steven's heart, solid and stable and comforting. He stands, pulls away for a step or two, but his legs wobble and his shoulder smacks into the side of the truck parked next to his. He crumples against the wheel well.

Fuck. Tell Steven the truth now, Hick God. Does Steven shame You? Does he grieve You? Steven wants to know, honestly. He's broke down again. He's retching in the bed of somebody else's truck. When You look at him, does Your gut wriggle? Do You want to close Your eyes? Do You want to spit Steven out, pour out Your wrath upon him, turn away and hide Your face? Answer Steven. You owe him a straight answer now. Steven's sick of mystery.

Do You struggle to love him? Do You love him?

Yes.

Steven's OK. He dabs his mouth as delicately as he can with the bandana he's knotted around his wrist, and then slips it off 'cause it itches. His eyes get stuck watching the moon glint off the streaked metal bottom of the bed.

Steven loves a truck bed. He's been touched gently in a truck bed. He'd ridden all the way west-young-man in a truck bed. More south-young-man from Corsicana maybe, but ain't got the same ring to it. He had to walk only half a mile from the house, follow the tracks to where Fifteenth Street curved, to hitch a ride. His stuff next to him, the paper bags crinkling with the wind on southbound 14, already past Wortham and Steven holding a ladder up off his legs with a bent knee. He'd gotten all the way to a rest stop north of town, past all the roadside motels on 35 and the wide-open smell of the spring burn, without really considering the choice he'd made, or that he'd made a choice at all. Steven was sixteen. Might could've crossed the highway and found a ride back, sure, and he was lost enough he might have, but the sun had gone down, and even from out there he could see the horizon glow a little, slightly, where the city must've been. The old guy driving came back with two Dr Peppers and a fresh pack of Lights, and Steven rode up front the rest of the way into Austin. Austin was just where you went. It was where a person went, when they needed someplace to go.

The moon warps and shimmies on the steel while Steven readies himself again. He picks something bitter and wet out of his teeth, an old piece of lime maybe. He stares as hard as he can at the still kernel of it under his fingernail until he finds his center of gravity. When he's this wasted, the center's always lower—a good bit lower—than he thinks it'll be.

If he's gonna get back before the end of the set, Steven needs to go now and fast. A few people are starting to sneak out the front door and the frame's staying lit—T.K. must have bricked it open already to get ready for the break. Steven can hear all the instruments slur together, the piano messy and mad, like somebody's laying on the keys and rolling around, so they're almost done for sure. He's gotta find Doug before he's overrun by fans. Just say *Hey, nice set,* and yeah, Steven's good.

Maybe he should run?

Don't, says Hick God. *Don't you even try. We'll take it one step at a time.*

Shut up, Hick God. You're underestimating Steven. It's hot still, night-hot and clammy, and You're an old, old dog; You pant and huff. And Steven can leave You in the dust tonight, once and for all.

But before Steven can drag himself more than a yard or two closer to the bar, he hears a voice in the mic—not Doug's but rougher, Joe's—say "Thanks, fuckers," and something else, and "tip your bartender," and then the music's gone.

The carpeted boom of a guitar hitting the stage. Nothing left but people's voices, and then they're streaming out the front and the side door into the sticky night, and Steven can't bring himself to come farther forward into the floodlights. He reaches for the whiskey, but his hand hits a long skid of crust on his T-shirt, some mess of dip and blood and old beer. His hair must look insane.

It's only when the crowd disperses that people seem dangerous to Steven. He loves a crowd, loves absolutely nothing more than soaking inside the warm, thronged cocoon of it. But when it breaks up into smaller clutches of people— when the music stops and there's nothing left to do but stand around and smoke, nothing left to watch but each other— Steven does sometimes get nervous. Walking back to the bar now, filthy and solo, feels like strolling into a pack of coyotes. They're lurking, quiet, toothy, and he can't do it. Not yet. He needs to clean himself up anyway, and after he does he'll sneak in the back and act like he was there the whole time.

He makes an abrupt left turn before anybody can clock him and stumbles down a row of bumpers in the direction of the creek instead.

It's muddier under his feet after he hits the tree line, softer, but then a hard old acorn stabs him right in the heel. He yelps faintly, but he keeps going. The mud's a good sign anyway—there's probably enough water in the creek to take a little gas-station bath, get to smelling a little better. And it's not far, maybe a minute's walk through the branches. The ground starts to slope and Steven slopes with it. He stops to light a smoke but can't, drops it before he can unearth a lighter. He takes a glug of his whiskey instead, and he hears it echo from somewhere in front of him, the sound of soft water as pretty as any song Steven knows. Yessir, there it is. Forward does always feel better to Steven than back. A boy's gotta do what he sets out to do.

That's a tree there, says Hick God, but it's too late. Steven swerves along the bark, falls. He pulls himself up to sitting, but it's hard to do and he's definitely sweating—he can feel the slick of dew on his skin, and there's a rank smell and a lot of something pooling in his mouth. He holds out his smoke-less hand and spits into it: a tooth. He spits again, and then he runs his tongue around to find the hole, and there's some ragged roots swimming in the bottom, but at least it's in the back of his mouth.

You want it, Lord? A small offering from Steven. He'll plant it here for You, deep deep deep down into the holy dirt, and maybe someday it'll blossom its own tiny little teeth. Steven likes this image. He files it away for Doug.

ey, brother," Doug had said to Steven last night, after he'd finally stopped talking about the music. Steven's hand was still on Doug's forearm, and he'd been drawing little circles on the taut skin with his index. Skimming back and forth over a vein like a road on a map. Steven's soft heart seeped up and all the way out into his fingertips, and he wondered if Doug could feel its voltage. Doug asked Steven if he was good—was he good, brother? But good was no word for what Steven was, his whole body beating.

"So good," Steven had said, maybe even out loud. Steven doesn't know. He's relying on Hick God to maintain the memorial record.

Steven looked around to make sure they were still totally alone, and then he got closer. Closer. Angled. Shivered. Then he put his lips on Doug's neck. He tasted Winston Lights and hot old tequila sweet as honeysuckle, and he exhaled as gently as he possibly could. He moved down toward the pretty collarbone, looked with his lips for the 4/4 of Doug's pulse. Up toward the earlobe then, by the temple, and a piece of salty blond hair in his open mouth, thicker than his own. Doug was still but for a sharp quiver of inhale, so Steven hadn't stopped. He didn't stop. He didn't.

I t's hard to get off the ground, but Steven manages to roll up onto his knees. His stomach roils like an ocean. He can't figure for a minute how he got here, looks up through the branches at the clouds migrating east. How'd Steven get here, Hick God?

Walked. Well, kinda.

No no, Hick God can do better than that. How'd Steven get here? How'd Steven do it, Hick God? His memory is a swamp. Why's he in the woods? Where's the band? Where's the music?

You can't look up like that, son, you're gonna fall again.

Steven looks down.

You came to wash up. But we can just go home, you know— still an option.

OK, wait a minute. Steven stands up. Where's home? He moves forward.

Wrong way, Hick God whispers, but Steven doesn't hear him. There's some strange note playing in his head—this kind of trebly, vibrating thing, like a high E-string with no warmth left in it, rusty and about to pure snap.

Can Steven tell You a story, Hick God? He's at the creek now and he's up to his anklebones in water. It feels like paradise flowing gold over his tore-up feet. It feels so good he sits full down in it. He cups the old rain in his hands and splashes it over his face, and up the back of his neck, and he feels cleaner than he has all day. He's finished the pint of whiskey, so he tosses the bottle and hears it shatter. He takes a sip of the creek too, but it's gritty and tastes shit-brown instead of blue.

Can Steven tell You a story? Once upon a time there was a boy named Steven. Right? See where it's going? *Calm down, son. Calm down.* Hark, Hick God! Steven's telling You a story. It's a good one. Once upon a time there was a boy named Steven, and a lot of people shut the book on him right then. But Steven was still there. Steven gathered all the strength he could gather and he, he. Shit, Steven's forgetting the story.

Once upon a time there was a boy named Steven. He needs to lie down again. Not here in the water, though, obviously. He backs himself up a few feet, up the bank where the ground's flatter. He'll take a short rest here. Steven will just wait for his clothes to dry a little, and then he'll go back inside to the music. He closes his swollen eyes. Listen, Hick God, lay him down easy. You're gonna have to finish the story. Once upon a time—

It's been twenty minutes. *Wake up,* Hick God says, down into Steven's ear canal. Hick God screeches and wheezes and wheedles the ugliest riff he can, a tune like a cheap fiddle sawing, until Steven wrenches open his eyes. *Wake up, Steven.* But Steven's lids are gauzy curtains, blowing open and closed again with barely a breeze. His face has opened up again, and it's leaking sludgy down one of his cheeks. He flips over onto his stomach, but it's too muddy to put his face against the ground, so he turns back over and settles where he was. His feet are up a little higher than his head, and it's like he's rocking in a hammock, a child on a swing.

Wake up, yells Hick God. *I can't finish the story without you.*

What story? Steven was dreaming. Even in his dream he was staggering.

R*emember, Steven, Doug's neck? Wake up.*
Doug had one hand still on the table, the other on the side of Steven's face. OK fine, Steven's awake. His hands are cold, he doesn't know why he's cold. He hadn't known if Doug's hand was pulling him in or holding him off, so Steven decided to push it and see. Steven slipped his tongue through his lips, under Doug's jawline, softened a couple days' worth of stubble. Doug was corpse-still. When Steven tried to crest the jaw, though, move to Doug's face, Doug pulled away. He leaned back against the vinyl of the chair and looked down at his lap. Steven needed and wanted and hoped. Steven was open wide. Doug could've reached out and touched the very inside of Steven, the squishy soul of Steven, and Steven ached with the possibility. He leaned in, lifted off the ground, and he put his forehead against Doug's, put his hand against Doug's chest so he wouldn't fall. He was so grateful he thought of Hick God, Steven did, as he leaned. He thought about all the ways he thought he'd been forsaken, and he felt Hick God's mercy thick in the air. Thank You, Hick God. Thank You for everything.

Yeah, sure, he heard a yell then from outside, and Doug jerked back, and Steven sat down so quick he hit the table. The guitar propped against it found the ground and all the notes went off at once, a hard ruin of noise right before the door swung open. T.K. was here to kick them out. Steven fussed with his hands like he'd been cleaning up, and Doug stood and moved out the door so jumpy his feet skipped off the floor. But when Steven got outside, it was bright as sunup. Nobody had unplugged the star, and the neon was sizzling as loud as Steven, and he was at the very beginning of the rest of his life.

Steven drifts off again. His mind is near blank, but he thinks he might be back inside. God, finally, he's made it back inside. He can hear the music and feel the crush of bodies against him. He's moving, dancing. All the brass is going in a big ole stampede, and a wet slip into the chorus. Steven's guts flutter, settle—flutter again, and settle. He's closer to Hick God than he's ever been, so close he can feel the hard callouses on Hick God's palms as they rub him. He can count the long Mississippis between Hick God's breaths. Hick God purrs and croons a soft song, and Steven feels it on his own lips. He hears a big major chord so syrupy Steven wants it to go on forever, and he's listening so close he doesn't even feel it when he gets sick, nope. He's out now and good. He gets sick again, there on his back. It's thin and he breathes it in, and the acid slides down his nose and his throat and fills his lungs steadily, like they're empty canteens. Sure, he'll forgive You, Hick God. Good of You to ask.

Steven has gone, is gone, long gone now, and with him his Hick God. There's nobody left at all, then, to see the sun come up. Nobody left to spot Doug's boy, hair a-flopping, snuck out his bed and running down the bank, face smooth and lit up with an easy glow from below his skin. If only Steven could see him. This kid coming at him. But there's nobody left to mistake this boy for that boy, for Steven in his long ago. Nobody left to hear the kid inhale sharp above Steven's body and then say *wow wow* as a short lick instead of words—a long, electric pause spun into the double thump of the kick drum. *Wow wow, wow wow.*

Doug won't play for a while—yeah, for a long time. He's gonna hurt. Every time he touches a fretboard he's gonna see Steven's long fingers instead of his. Deanna will feel responsible, but she'll suffer that sorrow somewhere else. The bar'll be back open on Friday, and Wendell will be standing behind it alone.

The story of Steven will last for everybody else too, but it'll morph and sweeten. It'll simplify. It'll straighten. It'll find a clearer progression—a couple clean, easy verses and a chorus in a key most people can carry. Round here, we like a past we can agree on. We'll pick whatever version we can sing all the way through, whatever song we can all sing together, and then, hey, we'll sing it.

ACKNOWLEDGMENTS

Thank you, *thank you*, to Lee Boudreaux, the best editor in this business, for seeing the potential in this story and helping—doggedly, patiently, delightfully—bring it to life. What a pleasure. To the rest of the team at Doubleday, especially Maya Pasic, Anne Jaconette, Julie Ertl, and Kayla Steinorth, for your beautiful work. To my agent, the beguiling PJ Mark, for your faith in me and your calming voice.

Thanks to the University of Michigan, Helen Zell, the Hopwood Foundation, and the Fine Arts Work Center in Provincetown for the time, space, and support. To all my teachers, most especially Peter Ho Davies and Claire Vaye Watkins, who are as brilliant with their students as they are on the page, and to Scotti Parrish, who saw this first and encouraged me to go on.

To the musicians whose cadences I crib and whose songs lunge at the divine: AM, BD, BW, CO, DS, EH, EITS, ES, JD, JI, JL, JM, JM, JTE, LW, NC, PG, SB, SN, SS, TVZ, WJ, WN, WS. For the inspiration and for the whiskey: Deep Eddy Cabaret, King Bee, the Continental, the White Horse, the Lost

Horse, Old Town, Cheer Ups, old Emo's on Red River, and the Longbranch Inn.

Thanks to the Michiganders, especially Mish Cheever, Nora and Colin Corrigan, Graham Cotten, Laura Lilly Cotten, Jeff Henebury, Clare Hogan, and Sylvan Thomson. To Nell Koring and Sam Krowchenko, for their weird, steadfast confidence in me and their sharp, sharp eyes. And to the Texans, especially Dalia Azim, Jennifer duBois, David Kalina for the early read, Marian Oman, Landon Sandy, Stacey Swann, Sasha West, and Liz Wyckoff.

To the men of the goddamn Cap City Cobras, for the absolute childlike joy and for letting me borrow their names. To Grace Coronado and Molly Shaw, for reminding me to kick a little and also the tattoos. To Jill Meyers, Adam Lefton, and Sofia Sokolove, for holding me up against the world. I hope you know.

And thank you to my family. Angus, the gentlest soul. Delaney and Erin, who see right through me and love me anyway. And to my parents, for their astonishing, unwavering support. They were both at the Armadillo in the '70s and so also very kindly fact-checked my cigarette brands. They gave me art and Texas. Every story I tell is for them.

This book was set in a typeface called Walbaum. The original cutting of this face was made by Justus Erich Walbaum (1768–1839) in Weimar in 1810. The type was revived by the Monotype Corporation in 1934. Young Walbaum began his artistic career as an apprentice to a maker of cookie molds. How he managed to leave this field and become a successful punch cutter remains a mystery. Although the type that bears his name may be classified as modern, numerous slight irregularities in its cut give this face its humane manner.